PICKLED TO DEATH

A Down South Café Mystery

Gayle Leeson

Grace Abraham Publishing
Bristol, Virginia

Gayle Leeson/Grace Abraham Publishing
13335 Holbrook Street, Suite 10
Bristol, Virginia 24202
www.gayleleeson.com

Publisher's Note: This is a work of fiction. Names, characters, places, and incidents are a product of the author's imagination. Locales and public names are sometimes used for atmospheric purposes. Any resemblance to actual people, living or dead, or to businesses, companies, events, institutions, or locales is completely coincidental.

Cover design by Wicked Smart Designs.

Book Layout ©2017 BookDesignTemplates.com

Ordering Information:
Quantity sales. Special discounts are available on quantity purchases by corporations, associations, and others. For details, contact the "Special Sales Department" at the address above.

Pickled to Death/Gayle Leeson. -- 1st ed.
ISBN 978-1-7373009-4-6

Dedicated to Tim, Lianna, and Nicholas

Chapter One

Clutching the steel bar in front of me as I stared down at the metal floor, I heard my boyfriend, Ryan, laugh beside me as the mechanical beast flung us into the air. Squeezing my eyes shut against the images spinning past as we careened around, I decided I owed Jackie an apology for teasing her about not wanting to ride the *Triggerman*. Hopefully, the feeling would pass when the ride stopped because I didn't want to hear my cousin's smug, *I told you so*.

The ride slowed and mercifully ended. Once my eyes settled back into their sockets, I glanced over at Ryan and smiled as we waited for the ride operator to come and release us from the restraints.

"Wasn't that great?" he asked.

Rather than lie, I said, "I'm looking forward to the *Scrambler*." Sure, that ride would sling us around, but it wouldn't have me feeling as if I were in training to be an astronaut.

"Yeah—but it'll feel tame compared to this."

Exactly. "It's always been my favorite."

Once the ride operator unbuckled us, I slipped my hand into Ryan's and took a wobbly step forward.

"Dudes! That was amazing!" Scott shouted, as he ambled toward us. "Didn't you love it? We should go again!"

Scott was a great guy who thought most things were amazing. He was also a server at my restaurant, the Down South Café. The whole gang had come out tonight. In addition to me, Ryan, and Scott; Jackie—my right hand at the café; Roger, her boyfriend; my best friend Sarah, and her boyfriend John had been eager to attend the first night of the fair. Luis, our busboy, was here with his family. We'd greeted them earlier while we were waiting for funnel cake.

I was regretting the funnel cake after the *Triggerman*, but I digress.

Winter Garden, Virginia, wasn't the most happening town; so when something as exciting as a fair came to town, almost everyone turned out to enjoy the novelty of it.

"We need to get over to the exhibit hall and see how Aunt Bess fared," I said.

Not only were we—with the exception of Jackie—here to enjoy the rides, but we were also here to support Aunt Bess, who'd entered the pickle-making competition.

Mabel Hobbs had won the contest for the past five years. And even though Aunt Bess had never competed, she'd entered her pickles this year because she felt the reigning "Big Dill" needed to be taken down a peg or two.

I'd been surprised upon arriving at Mom's house last week and asking, "Where's Aunt Bess?"

"You'll have to see it to believe it," Mom had said.

She'd led me into the kitchen where Aunt Bess was placing cucumber spears into jars.

"What are you doing?" I asked Aunt Bess.

"I'm making pickles for the fair." She raised her chin and gave me a look of defiance. "I'm throwing my hat in the ring." With a nod of satisfaction, she crammed more cucumber slices into the jars. "Well, I'm throwing my *pickles* into the ring—not my hat. Though I imagine I could make a pretty hat, if I put my mind to it."

"You're entering the pickle competition?" I looked from Aunt Bess to Mom and back again. Aunt Bess had hung up her apron years ago. She now cajoled the rest of us into preparing whatever food she wanted.

"Yes, I am," Aunt Bess said. "I was over at the beauty parlor yesterday, and Mabel Hobbs came in bragging that the mayor had called her Winter Garden's Pickle Queen and said that nobody could hold a candle to her when it came to pickle-making. Well, by crackies, I'm fixing to show her that I can."

So, here we were getting ready to enter the exhibition hall to see if Aunt Bess had managed to unseat Mabel Hobbs. I wasn't sure what I wanted the outcome to be. If Aunt Bess lost, she'd swear up and down she was cheated and would sulk for days. If she won, she'd be insufferable and—even worse—might decide to take up cooking again.

"The mail carrier told me at work today that Daphne Martin Jacobs has set up a beautiful display in the exhibit hall," Sarah said. "I can hardly wait to see it."

"Me, too." Scott grinned. "As soon as we see Aunt Bess's pickles, I'm scoping out Daphne's display."

I heard a piercing whistle and turned to see Roger waving his arm at us. Mom and Clark were standing with him and Jackie.

"Have fun?" Jackie asked, when we joined them.

"It was…um…exhilarating. You should give it a try." I turned to Mom. "Is Aunt Bess already in there?"

She nodded. "I'm half afraid to go see how she fared."

"I was thinking the same thing." I took Mom's arm and smiled up at Clark as we walked. He was the town's only doctor. "You wouldn't happen to have any mild sedatives on you, would you?"

"Do you really think we'll need them?" he asked.

Inclining my head, I answered, "Well, I'd imagine elephant tranquilizers might be more appropriate, but those would be overkill."

"Not by much," Mom muttered. "If she loses, I'm running off to Tahiti for a week."

"And if she wins?" Clark asked.

"A month." She winked. "Wanna go?"

Before he could answer, a large, sweaty, naked man burst through the door of the exhibit hall and ran past us.

My jaw dropped. "Did I just see what I thought I saw?"

"Yep," Jackie said.

Two security guards rushed out after the—well, the exhibitionist—and paused long enough for one of them to ask, "Which way did he go?"

I jerked my thumb over my shoulder.

"Why?" Sarah asked. "Just *why*?"

"I suppose I should help the guards." Ryan was looking in the direction the trio had ran, but he didn't seem inclined to help.

"You're off duty," I said. "Besides, it's not like the naked guy had a gun or anything."

"That's—"

A scream permeated the air, followed by another and then the cacophony of a panicked crowd.

Ryan brushed past us and hurried into the building. "Stay here until I can find out what's happening," he called over his shoulder.

"Aunt Bess," Mom said softly.

"Granny!" Jackie raced through the door behind Ryan.

"I might be needed." Clark muscled through the tide of people who were now pouring through the double doors of the building.

"And Aunt Bess might need us." I looked at Mom. "You stay—"

"The heck I will."

Glancing around at the rest of our group, I could see they were as determined as Mom and me to get inside and make sure Aunt Bess was all right.

We were jostled around by the crowd quite a bit, but we finally made it into the throng surrounding the pickle competition booth. Aunt Bess was standing off to the side beside Ryan, who was talking on his cell phone. There were several other security guards and officers nearby. Clark and a paramedic were crouched beside someone. Craning my neck, I could see it was Mabel Hobbs. She was lying on the concrete floor in an ever-widening pool of blood and pickle juice. A broken jar near her head indicated she'd been bashed over the head with her batch of first-prize winning pickles. The blue ribbon lay near the body.

Jackie managed to break through and get to Aunt Bess and envelop her in a hug. "Granny, what happened? Are you all right?"

"Excuse us," I said loudly, "we're with the police." Technically, we were. Ryan was the police, and we were here with him. Grabbing Mom's arm, I pulled her with me over to where Aunt Bess, Ryan, and Jackie were standing.

"I don't know what happened," Aunt Bess was saying. "I turned around to watch the streaker like everybody else—even though that whole incident was a disappointment." She scoffed. "I reckon the people you'd actually *want* to see running around nude would never do such a thing, would they?"

"But what about Mabel Hobbs?" Mom asked.

Aunt Bess screwed up her face. "Ugh, no! Who'd want to see Mabel in her birthday suit?"

They were joined by a uniformed deputy before Mom could clarify her question. After speaking to Ryan, the deputy turned to Aunt Bess. "Can you tell me what happened here?"

I'd never met the deputy before, but I was guessing he was taking charge of the situation.

"I was giving Mabel Hobbs a piece of my mind when I heard a commotion going on in the middle of the exhibit hall, and I looked to see what was going on," she said. "It was that streaker. When I realized he was nothing to write home about, I turned back to Mabel; but there she was lying on the floor. Somebody must've hit her over the head with that jar of pickles yonder." She pointed out the broken jar in case the deputy had missed it.

"Witnesses saw you and the victim arguing just prior to the disturbance," he said.

"Honey, it *was* disturbing, wasn't it? The whole shebang. First of all, Mabel got the daylights knocked out of her before I could finish telling her what a cheat I think she is, and the streaker wasn't anybody I'd want to see without his clothes on. Why, I remember back in the seventies when that sort of thing was in its heyday—"

"Tell me more about the argument you were having with Ms. Hobbs," the deputy interrupted.

"Oh, that. I believe she buys her pickles from the grocery store and then puts them in her own jars to enter into the competition, and I told her so. Somebody needs to look into that and disqualify her—you know, after they get her head bandaged up."

"Did you break that jar of pickles over the victim's head?" he asked.

"Hey, you wait just a minute!" Jackie stepped in front of Aunt Bess. "My granny wouldn't—"

Roger stepped closer to Jackie. "Let Aunt Bess answer the question. She can tell him herself that she didn't do anything wrong."

"Thank you, Roger." Aunt Bess lifted her chin. "Jackie is right, though. I'd never have hit Mabel with her pickles—I need them for evidence that she cheated. Let's just hope she has another jar stashed somewhere and that we can use those to prove they're store bought. Besides, you can't haul off and smack a body in the head with a thick glass jar like that—especially somebody old like Mabel—it's liable to kill her."

I caught Clark giving the paramedic a slight shake of his head. He straightened, and the two men spoke quietly for a moment before the paramedic and his partner loaded Mabel Hobbs onto a gurney and carried her through the back exit of the building.

Clark came over to where we were standing. "I'm going to accompany the paramedics to the hospital."

"I hope Mabel will be okay," Aunt Bess said.

"I need to take you down to the station and get a formal statement from you," the deputy told Aunt Bess.

"A formal statement?" She frowned. "I've already told you everything I know."

"I don't think that's necessary this evening," Ryan said. "Sheriff Billings is a personal friend of the family, and I'm sure he'd prefer to question the witness himself."

The deputy's jaw tightened. "I'll call and ask him about that."

"Please do." Ryan turned to us. "Let's go."

As we were walking out, Sarah and John flanked Aunt Bess. Sarah worked for the only attorney in town, and John was in law school.

Ryan took my hand, and I gave him a grateful smile.

"Sorry you didn't get to ride the Scrambler," he whispered.

"That's okay. I believe I'm scrambled enough as it is."

Chapter Two

I hadn't slept well, so I felt kinda like a sleepwalker when I arrived at the café the next morning. My first order of business was to get the coffee made. After readying the pots—one dark roast, one French vanilla, and one decaf—I went into the kitchen and put a batch of cinnamon buns into the oven. Scott had made them yesterday afternoon so that all I had to do when I got here was bake them.

With those tasks done, I returned to the dining room, leaned against the counter, and waited for the coffee to percolate. While I waited, I looked around the café to see if anything else needed to be done. Everything appeared to be in order. The floors were swept, the tables were clean, the napkin dispensers and salt and pepper shakers were filled.

I was proud of the Down South Café. When I'd bought it, it had been called Lou's Joint. Besides the name, I'd been eager to change the décor. With the help of Roger and his construction crew, the café had gone from dingy browns and oranges to cheerful blues and yellows. He'd replaced the cracked linoleum with bamboo flooring, and he'd even built a screened-in patio for patrons to enjoy when the weather cooperated.

A police cruiser pulled into the parking lot, and I smiled slightly. Ryan must be coming to check on me—and Aunt Bess—after last night. As the car got closer, I could see that Sheriff Billings was driving.

While I wasn't sure why the sheriff was coming to visit, I did know both men would welcome a cup of coffee. All three pots had finished brewing. I poured French vanilla for myself and dark roast for both men.

"Good morning," Sheriff Billings said, as he came through the door. "Nothing more lovely than a pretty woman offering you a cup of coffee, is there, deputy?"

"Not when that woman is Amy." Ryan winked.

"You've managed to beat the rest of my staff to work this morning, but I'll be happy to make you some breakfast," I said, ignoring the compliments. Flattery was often a tool, even if it was used merely to soften a blow. I wanted them to tell me why they were here.

"I don't want to put you to any trouble." The sheriff sat at the counter. "But do I smell cinnamon rolls baking?"

"Yes. They'll be done soon."

"I'd like one of those too," Ryan said.

The oven timer dinged. I went into the kitchen, quickly made the frosting, iced the cinnamon rolls, plated two, and brought them back out to Ryan and the sheriff.

Handing them each a napkin-wrapped set of silverware, I asked, "Are you ready to tell me why you're here so early?"

"We hoped to talk with you about your great-aunt." Sheriff Billings unwrapped his silverware and used the side of his fork to cut into the cinnamon roll. "Did she say anything about Mabel Hobbs after she got home last night?"

"Nothing she hadn't already said to the deputy who questioned her at the fair," I said. "What are your other witnesses saying?"

"You know we can't discuss an ongoing investigation." The sheriff took a sip of coffee. "But I can tell you I'm treating Aunt Bess as a witness rather than a suspect—at least, at this time."

"What about the streaker?" I looked from the sheriff to Ryan. "It can't have been purely coincidental that he created a disturbance at exactly the time Mabel Hobbs was hit over the head."

Inclining his head, the sheriff said, "It might have been coincidental on the streaker's part—Mabel Hobbs' killer could have simply used the distraction to his or her advantage—or the streaker might've been an active participant in the murder." He took a bite of the cinnamon roll. "This is delicious."

"Thanks." I didn't mention the fact that Scott had made them—they weren't going to get me off track that easily.

"It's difficult to speculate about what role the streaker might have played without having questioned him," Ryan said.

"So, you haven't caught him yet?" I asked.

"'Fraid not." Ryan sipped his coffee. "We're pursuing every lead. Unfortunately, there were no security cameras in the exhibit hall."

"Or fortunately, from what I've heard." The sheriff shook his head and dug back into his cinnamon roll.

"Still, somebody in that crowd is bound to have recognized him." I frowned. "When are you planning to question Aunt Bess?"

"After we leave here," Ryan said.

"You'd better take her a cinnamon roll then."

"Make it two." Sheriff Billings gave me a brief smile.

Ryan and the sheriff were leaving when Scott and Luis came into work.

"Are we late?" Luis asked, looking up at the clock over the serving hatch.

Shaking my head, I said, "No, they were really early."

"Were they here about what happened last night?" Scott asked.

"Yes." I jerked my head toward the kitchen, so they'd know to follow me. I needed to do my breakfast prep work. "They're on their way to question Aunt Bess now."

Both Scott and Luis stopped.

"They're not going to arrest her, are they?" Scott asked.

"Question her?" Luis gaped at me. "What do they think she did?"

As I put biscuit ingredients into the mixer, I explained to Luis that Aunt Bess had been standing over Mabel Hobbs after Ms. Hobbs had been hit with her jar of prize-winning pickles. "Ms. Hobbs died as a result of her injuries."

"But they don't think Aunt Bess did it, do they?" he asked.

"I'll cover for you." Scott took the mixing cup filled with butter from my hands. "You need to get over to the big house."

Most of my friends and I referred to my mom's house as "the big house." My grandparents had lived there, Aunt

Bess had moved in with Nana after my grandfather died, and then Mom moved in with Aunt Bess when Nana passed. I lived in the guest house down the hill from the big house.

Taking back the butter, I said, "It's all right. They're not going to harass her or anything, and the sheriff assured me he's going to question Aunt Bess as a witness rather than a suspect." I spooned the butter into the mixing bowl. "Besides, Mom is there."

"If you're sure…" Scott got some apples from the pantry.

"I am. Mom will let me know if I'm needed." I smiled. "But I appreciate the offer."

"Anytime. I'm going to make a batch of apple muffins unless there's something else you need me to do."

"That's fine," I said.

Luis began topping off the condiment bottles.

The café smelled wonderful when Dilly and Walter strolled in and sat at the counter.

"What smells so good?" Dilly asked.

"It could be my apple muffins," Scott said, with a grin.

"I'll try one of those," Dilly said, "but don't forget Buddy's biscuit—plain, please—I'll put some jam on it later."

"I'll have an apple muffin too," her husband, Walter, said. "But I'd also like two scrambled eggs, two sausage patties, and a biscuit with gravy."

"Well, in that case, I'll have the same thing Walter is having." She gave Scott a decisive nod. "But with the extra biscuit for the raccoon."

"Are you sure you don't want me to put the jam on Buddy's biscuit for you?" I teased.

Dilly had always given the raccoon who came out of the woods to her back porch every evening a plain biscuit until I'd fed him while she and Walter were on their honeymoon. The little mooch got picky after that and wouldn't eat plain biscuits anymore.

"I can manage." She rolled her eyes. "I hate I missed all the excitement at the fair last night. Walter and I were waiting to go tonight because we like the band that's playing."

"Who's going to be there?" Luis asked.

"Sawyer Sykes." Dilly shook her head. "He's a talented singer, but I'm afraid he can't top a streaker and a murder. We always manage to miss the excitement."

Sawyer Sykes? Why would he ever come back to Winter Garden?

"That's not necessarily a bad thing," Walter said. "Scott, how are you doing?"

I whisked the eggs. That wasn't a very subtle change of subject, but I was glad Walter had provided it. I knew that all day patrons would be discussing Mabel Hobbs' death. I just hoped they wouldn't be speculating about whether or not Aunt Bess was the one who bashed the woman over the head.

Who am I kidding? Of course, they will be. I only hope it won't be where Jackie or I can hear it.

Jackie had class until eleven-thirty this morning, but she was planning to come in afterward. I realized I should probably text her and tell her she ought to stay with Aunt Bess.

Does Mom know Sawyer is in town?

They'd dated and become pretty serious before he'd taken off like a hound on a rabbit's trail. As far as I knew, he'd never looked back. Until now.

I wished I had some way to put my thoughts on hold, at least until I could get Walter and Dilly's breakfast finished.

Tuning back into the conversation taking place at the counter, I heard Scott saying, "—an advanced cake decorating class with Daphne Martin Jacobs in Brea Ridge after work."

"Wait, what?" I poked my head through the server hatch. "You didn't tell me you'd signed up for a cake decorating class."

"I wanted to surprise you with my mad skills, Amy-girl." He grinned. "But it starts today, and I got excited and blabbed to my man, Walter."

"I think you're an awesome cake decorator already, but I can hardly wait to see how you expand on your skillset. Let me pay for the class," I said.

"Nah. I couldn't do that. Besides, what if I fail?"

Dilly scoffed. "We have every ounce of confidence in you. And Daphne knows her stuff. I've had her do cakes for me before—that was before I knew you, Scott."

"What will you be learning in this class?" Walter asked. "Do you need a taste tester?"

"I probably will, dude. The classes will be every Tuesday for a month. The first thing I'm learning is how to paint on cake. I'm taking a six-inch, double-layer cake to class. I got up and baked it this morning. After work, I'm going to crumb coat it and then put it back in the fridge until time for class."

"Do you need a pastry box?" I asked. "There are plenty in the back."

"I'll take you up on that. Thanks."

"I can hardly wait to see what you come in with tomorrow," Dilly said. "You *will* bring it so we can see it, won't you?"

"Darling, don't put the young man on the spot." Walter patted Dilly's hand.

"I don't mind," Scott said. "Even if it's not very good, I'll bring it in. No matter how ugly it'll be, it'll still taste good."

"I'm sure your cake will be fabulous." I flipped the sausage patties. "You have a gift."

Jackie came into work in the middle of the breakfast rush.

"Was your class canceled?" I asked.

"No." She tied on her *Down South Café* apron and didn't even look over at me.

"Jackie, what's wrong?"

"I didn't go to class, okay?"

"No, it's not okay. Why are you acting this way?"

She took a deep breath. "I spent the night with Granny, so I'd be there when the police questioned her—or whatever—this morning."

"All right. Did something happen during the—" I didn't want to call it an *interrogation*. "—the interview?"

"Yeah. Sheriff Billings got a call. A witness has come forward to say she saw Granny hit Mabel Hobbs with that pickle jar."

Chapter Three

Since Jackie didn't know anything more, and since the breakfast rush was in full swing, we had to table the discussion until later. It was awfully hard to work with the questions tripping over each other in my brain:

Who is this witness? Could she be the person who actually murdered Mabel Hobbs? Did she think Aunt Bess would be the perfect scapegoat? If this witness isn't the killer, what had she seen to make her believe Aunt Bess smashed Mabel Hobbs over the head with her prize-winning pickles? Surely—?

No. I couldn't entertain that thought. Not for a second. I was absolutely positive Aunt Bess was innocent. Of course, it was impossible to be absolutely positive about anything, right? But I was ninety-nine percent certain that

Aunt Bess had not whacked Mabel Hobbs with that pickle jar. Ninety-eight percent, minimum.

I poured pancake batter onto the griddle and prayed Aunt Bess's ordeal would be over soon.

By the time Homer Pickens came in at a quarter past ten, the crowd had dwindled. There was one customer paying Scott at the register and one other—Madelyn Carver—still enjoying her brunch.

Homer was something of an eccentric. He came into the café every morning to have a sausage biscuit and coffee at promptly ten-thirty. Since he also had a new hero every day and could quote these heroes extensively, I was convinced he had a photographic memory.

His typically cheerful face was drawn as he sat on his favorite stool.

"Hi, Homer," I said. "Everything all right?"

"I reckon." His sigh contradicted his words. "I simply have to remember the words of today's hero, Sir John Lubbock. 'In this world, we do not see things as they are. We see them as we are because what we see depends mainly on what we're looking for.'"

Jackie's eyes widened, and she hurried over from the register. "You know something. Homer, what do you know?"

"I don't know anything."

Scott and Luis joined Jackie and me at the counter, and I could've sworn I saw Madelyn's ears perk up as well.

Madelyn was a paralegal in an Abingdon law firm, but she was able to work from home two days a week. On most of those days, she ate brunch here; and when I was running low on Landon Farms honey to sell, she brought some in. Today, she was here for French toast…and, apparently, a little gossip.

"Homer, what is it?" I asked gently.

"On the way here, I stopped to talk with Pete at the bookstore. Ellen Hurley came in and said she saw Maude and Earl Ennis over at the municipal building this morning." He gulped.

I got him a glass of water as well as his usual cup of dark roast coffee.

"Thanks," he said. "Ellen had been to the post office, and she ran into Maude and Earl in the parking lot."

Jackie blew out a breath, and I gave her a warning glance. If she upset Homer, he wouldn't tell us anything.

Glancing nervously at his rapt audience, Homer continued. "Maude told Ellen she was fixing to talk with the sheriff to give her report. She—" He cleared his throat. "She said she saw a woman commit a murder last night."

I raised my eyes to Jackie's once again. "Well, now we know who the witness is."

Neither Scott nor Luis—or Madelyn, for that matter—knew anything about a witness, so I quickly filled them in.

Raising her hand to her throat, Jackie asked, "Is Granny going to be arrested?"

"Maybe this Maude chick did the deed," Scott said. "What better way to cover her tracks than for her to say she saw someone else do it?"

"Scott has a point," Homer said. "And Maude has never struck me as a kindhearted person."

"I saw on TV that eyewitness statements are the most unreliable pieces of evidence," Luis said. "So, who cares what she saw? We know Aunt Bess is innocent."

"This Ennis lady could have a grudge against your Aunt Bess too." Madelyn stood and joined us at the counter. "It would be worth digging into. Amy, I know you're good at digging."

I couldn't deny that I'd poked my nose into her father's death. But then, how could I not have? He died in my parking lot! Plus, I'd helped the police find his killer.

Madelyn walked over to the counter to pay. Scott went to help her, and I hurried into the kitchen to make Homer's sausage biscuit. I was running behind and needed to step it up if I was going to have it ready by his usual ten-thirty.

Homer had just finished his second cup of coffee and was getting ready to leave when I saw Mom and Aunt

Bess driving up to the café. There was a couple having brunch on the patio, but there were no other customers, besides Homer, in the dining room.

Jackie hadn't noticed them yet, so I eased over to the display case where she was putting a fresh batch of chocolate chip cookies.

"Mom and Aunt Bess are coming," I said, softly. "Don't overreact. If you treat Aunt Bess like she's a victim or like the police are targeting her, then she'll feel that way too."

Jackie glared at me. "I believe I know my grandmother better than you do." She took the cookie sheet back into the kitchen.

"Don't take her behavior to heart," Homer whispered. "She's concerned and likely didn't sleep well last night. It's as Sir John Lubbock said, 'A day of worry is more exhausting than a week of work.' She'll feel better after seeing her grandmother and getting some reassurance from her."

I nodded. "Thanks, Homer."

Mom opened the door for Aunt Bess, who strolled in as if she were a celebrity.

"Hi, everybody!" Aunt Bess came over to the counter and patted Homer on the shoulder. "How've you been, Homer?"

"Very well, Bess. I appreciate your asking."

Jackie came out and hugged Aunt Bess. "Granny, are you all right? What did the sheriff say? He'd better not try to pin Mabel Hobbs' attack on you."

"Take a breath, darlin'." She smiled. "You're more upset about this ordeal than I am."

I looked at Mom, who gave me a shrug.

"Of course, I'm sorry about poor, old Mabel," Aunt Bess continued, "but nobody truly thinks I whacked her. As I pointed out last night, I wouldn't have destroyed my sole piece of evidence that Mabel cheated her way to that blue ribbon for anything."

"We heard there was a witness who said she saw you holding the jar," Jackie said.

Aunt Bess waved her granddaughter's concerns away with the flick of her wrist. "That old Maude Ennis. She never did have the good sense the Lord gave a milk cow. Granted, she saw me holding Mabel's pickle jar up over my head but not because I was fixing to bash it over Mabel's head. I was holding it up to the light and pointing out all those little black peppercorns in the bottom of the jar. They're what proved to me that those pickles were store-bought."

"Did anyone take the jar from you?" I asked.

"No. I put it back down on the table so I could go find a judge. But then the streaker came running out—"

"Some people have no sense of propriety." Homer sighed.

"That's true, but you didn't miss anything worth looking at, I assure you," Aunt Bess told him. "When I turned back around to Mabel to tell her I was going to seek out a judge, she was lying there at my feet."

I drummed my fingers on the counter. "Who else was standing by the table?"

"Nobody after the streaker ran by."

"But who was there before?" Mom asked.

"Oh, several people were wandering by. You already know Maude Ennis was there nosing into everybody's business, so her husband, Earl, probably wasn't too far away. Mabel's stepchildren, Bella and Drew, were there at some point. There was a nice-looking man with them. I believe he must've been Bella's fella." She chuckled. "See what I did there? I think his name was Mark."

"What kind of relationship did Mabel appear to have with Bella and Drew?" I asked.

"Contentious," Aunt Bess said.

"That's common knowledge," Homer added. "Mabel's husband, Ralph, died last year, and I imagine his children were waiting for Mabel to join him in the Great Beyond so they could inherit."

I frowned. "So, Mabel and Ralph didn't have any children together?"

Homer shook his head.

"Drew and Bella weren't the only ones ticked at Mabel last night. She'd caught William Fairley stealing t-shirts when one of the vendor's backs was turned, and she'd made it clear to Will that she was going to rat him out to the police as soon as she got rid of me."

There were plenty of people who had reason to want Mabel Hobbs out of the picture—three of which were standing around the pickle table last night before Mabel was killed. I felt like another visit to the fair was in order.

Chapter Four

Jackie was spending the evening with Aunt Bess again, so I asked Sarah to accompany me to the fair. As we walked along the midway, aromas of popcorn and fried dough wafted on the air. I looked over at the *Triggerman* as we passed and smiled slightly at the squeals of delight—or terror—rising above the rock music accompanying the ride.

"You wanna give it another whirl since we're here?" Sarah asked.

"No! I mean, not unless you do."

She laughed. "No, I don't need to experience that thing again either."

"Keep an eye out for the streaker," I said.

"You don't think he'd be so bold as to make a repeat appearance, do you?" she asked. "Not now that the police are looking for him and wondering if he's somehow involved in Mabel Hobbs' death."

"I doubt it, but you never know." I nodded toward the exhibit hall. "Let's go take a better look at the exhibits."

To the right, there was a display case with beautifully decorated cakes created by Daphne Jacobs. There was a sign above the case reading Daphne's Delectable Cakes and a stack of flyers advertising Daphne's cake decorating classes as well as her services as a baker.

Inside the case was a sculpted cake in the shape of a mother otter with her baby on her stomach. That one made us say, Aww. There was a five-tier white and Wedgewood blue wedding cake with intricate string work. A gorgeous Victorian house made from gingerbread was decorated with tiny candies and delicate royal icing. Finally, there was a three-tier cake on which Daphne had painted Monet's water lilies.

"Wow," Sarah said. "She does impressive work."

"Doesn't she? Scott is taking her cake painting class. That's what he's doing this evening as a matter of fact."

"How cool. I wish I could be more of a crafter." She winked. "But then I get over it."

I linked my arm through hers as we strolled on to look at the winning cakes submitted for the competition. The white-ribbon winner was a three-dimensional cake in the form of a jack-o-lantern. Second place went to a cake decorated to look like a basket of flowers. The blue-ribbon cake was a labradoodle puppy.

"That's gorgeous, but who could cut it?" Sarah laughed. "I'd feel so guilty slicing into such a realistic looking dog."

"Me too. I think it's the eyes. They make it look so lifelike."

There were several other pretty cakes, but Sarah and I agreed that the three winners deserved their ribbons. It wasn't until we got away from the cakes that we began to question the judging.

Our misgivings began with the biscuits. Some were fluffier than others. The third-place winner appeared to be slightly overdone. The second-place biscuit looked okay, but the winner was too flat.

"Why did that one win?" Sarah asked, looking around to make sure no one else had heard her. "It's flatter than a postage stamp."

"I don't know. Maybe the taste was better?" I doubted it, though. A biscuit that flat was likely not properly mixed or the baker hadn't used enough baking powder.

We moved on to the photography exhibit. All the photographs were interesting—some especially pretty—and we realized art was subjective. While we couldn't see what raised the three winners above the rest of the entries, we decided to go on the assumption that the judges knew what they were doing.

That assumption went completely out the window when we saw the drawing entries. The third-place winner was breathtaking. It was a portrait of an elderly couple—the man was kissing his wife on the cheek. The couple seemed as if they might speak or laugh at any second.

Sarah raised her hand to her mouth. "That's incredible. If that's third place, I can hardly wait to see what won first and second."

My jaw dropped. "No. Way."

The second-place winner looked as if it had been drawn in the dark, possibly by a cat, and the first-place winner was even worse.

"What?" Sarah forgot to use her inside voice.

"Shh!"

"No, no, no. I will not shush. Do you know how angry I'd be if I drew that—" She pointed to the portrait bearing the third-place ribbon. "—and I lost to those?"

"Maybe the judges thought the third-place winner was traced or something," I said.

"Then in that case, the drawing should have been disqualified." She shook her head. "I think Aunt Bess might've been onto something. It's possible—even likely—these exhibits weren't judged fairly."

Before I could voice my agreement, there was an announcement about the band getting ready to start.

"Let's walk on over and see Sawyer Sykes for about five minutes while we ponder what, if anything, we can do to question the judges' competence."

"Five minutes?" She snorted. "You don't think you're going to like the band?"

"I know I don't like the man," I said. "I just want to see if my mom is here."

She was. Front row. No sign of Aunt Bess, Clark, or any of Mom's friends. She was flying solo.

I groaned. "Darn it."

"Spill," Sarah said.

"My mom dated Sawyer about fifteen years ago, and he broke her heart. Now I'm afraid she's going to make a huge mistake."

Sawyer grinned at Mom as he began crooning a ballad. I ground my teeth and wished he'd suffer a sudden attack of laryngitis.

From the right of the stage, a large man—naked but this time wearing jogging shoes and a Mardi Gras mask while shining as if he'd been drenched in baby oil—took off running. It was the same streaker as last night. As he sprinted through the crowd, oil and sweat flying off his body, three security officers chased after him. One officer skidded and fell. One managed to grab the man but couldn't hold onto his greasy body. The last I saw, the third man was still giving chase.

Sawyer Sykes' band abandoned the ballad and began playing the Ray Stevens' classic *The Streak*. Was it a coincidence that the group had the song in their repertoire? Or had the stunt been planned? Maybe the streaker had done his test run last night to get people talking and to generate interest in returning to the fair tonight. It was worth looking into, and I certainly planned to confide my suspicions—about Sawyer Sykes and the judging—to Ryan.

Sarah and I managed to sit through the concert, which probably wouldn't have been so bad had it been someone I didn't dislike so thoroughly. Afterwards, I hurried to join Mom.

"Hey!" I smiled. "Sarah and I are going to have some milkshakes. Want to join us?"

"No, thanks."

"We're not going anywhere special—just back to my house." I played my trump card. "You know how Princess Eloise misses you, and she hasn't seen you in a few days."

Princess Eloise was the white Persian cat mom had to leave with me because Aunt Bess was allergic.

"I'll try to get down there tomorrow. I have plans."

I turned to Sarah. "Let's go."

When we got to my car—a yellow bug my grandmother had bought me when I turned sixteen—she asked, "Wanna talk about it?"

Sighing, I said, "Sawyer Sykes left my mom because he clearly hadn't wanted to be saddled with raising a middle-schooler. Truth be told, he probably didn't want to be saddled with a wife either. I think he's likely the kind of cowboy who prefers a different saddle for every day of the week. And now Mom is going to blow her relationship with a terrific man for this…this—"

"Saddler," Sarah finished.

"Exactly." I opened the door and slid behind the wheel.

"Your mom knows what she's doing," Sarah said, as she got into the car. "Trust her."

"That's easier said than done."

"Mm-hmm. I imagine she thought the same thing about you on occasion."

I glared at her. "Take that back, or no caramel in your milkshake."

She held up her hands in surrender.

After Sarah left, I cuddled on the sofa with Rory, my brown terrier. Princess Eloise wasn't big on snuggling, but she lay on the arm of the sofa for moral support. Both pets could sense I was in a state of unease.

I took out my phone and called Ryan.

"Hello, beautiful. Did you have a good evening?"

"Not especially." I told him my suspicions about the streaker being paid to drum up business for Sawyer Sykes. "It struck both Sarah and me very odd that the band knew the Ray Stevens' song so well—and that everyone in the band immediately began playing it—as soon as the streaker made his appearance."

"One of our officers who was there also thought the production was staged," he said. "He went to talk with the band after the concert, but Sawyer ducked out with some woman."

I cringed. This wouldn't be the best time to tell him that the woman Sawyer left with was probably my mom. Besides, I could be wrong. I doubted it, since her SUV wasn't up at the big house yet, but I could still hope.

"The band members agreed to come into the station tomorrow morning," Ryan continued.

"That streaker wasn't the only strange thing at the fair. Sarah and I believe Aunt Bess could be right about the judging not being on the level." I told him about some of the exhibits we saw.

"My mom said the same thing, but I thought she was simply angry because Hilda Dinsmore won a blue ribbon, and she got a red one."

"I'm going to see if I can get a meeting with Daphne Jacobs to see what the officials might have told her about the judging procedures."

We talked for a while longer, and then I got up and went into the kitchen for a drink of water. Still no sign of Mom at the big house. I called her but got her voicemail. I supposed I could call Jackie to see if she'd heard anything from Mom. But I didn't want to disturb her and Aunt Bess. And, more likely, I didn't want confirmation of what I already knew—that my mother was rekindling her romance with that snake, Sawyer Sykes.

Chapter Five

Scott's head was high, and his chest was puffed out a little as he carried his painted cake into the café on Wednesday morning. Luis held the door for him and looked almost as proud as Scott—and, as far as I knew, Luis hadn't even seen the cake yet. That's a sign of true friendship.

"Get in here and open up that box!" I exclaimed. "I can hardly wait to see what you've made!"

"It's a first effort," Scott said. "Remember, that was only my first class yesterday evening."

"I know that—we all know that." I looked around at Jackie, silently daring her to say anything negative if the cake wasn't terribly pretty. My cousin could be critical, not to hurt but to help. Just…sometimes it didn't help.

He placed the pastry box on the counter, opened it, and took out the small white cake upon which he'd painted Van Gogh's sunflowers.

I gasped. "If this is a first effort, what are you going to do when you get really good? This is gorgeous, Scott."

"Aw, you're just being nice." He pointed. "See right here where I smudged the gold into the brown?"

"No," Jackie said. "No one sees that. All we see is a beautiful cake."

"Yeah," Luis said. "That looks too good to eat. If I'd worked that hard on something and someone cut it up, I'd be kinda ticked."

Scott took out his phone. "You think mine is nice, wait until you see Leslie's." He turned the screen around to show us a photo of a light blue cake with Japanese cherry blossoms climbing up the side.

"That is pretty," I said, "but I think yours is better."

"You're biased." Scott grinned.

"Who's Leslie?" Luis asked.

"She's Daphne's niece, and she's something special." He swiped onto another photo. "Here's one of her with her cake."

"Wow." Luis gave a low whistle. "Did you get her number?"

Scott's cheeks reddened. "Dude, I'll see her next week in class."

His relief was palpable when Dilly and Walter arrived, and attention turned back to his cake.

"Oh, Scott, honey, this is extraordinary!" Dilly got out her phone and started snapping photos. "I'll be sure to show the women in my Bible study class this evening, and they're gonna be ringing your phone off the hook."

"Are you sure you made that?" Walter asked, giving Scott a mock look of suspicion. "That's not the teacher's demo, is it?"

Scott laughed. "Nope. If you look closely, you'll see all my mistakes."

"We've tried to tell him we don't see any mistakes," Jackie said. "I think he's fishing for compliments. Scott, that's the ugliest cake any of us have ever seen. Let's eat it."

"Burned by the Jackster!" Scott shouted.

"What have I told you about the nicknames?" she asked.

He merely grinned and went into the kitchen for a cake knife.

"Did you guys make it to the fair last night?" I asked.

"Yes," Dilly said. "Did you go?"

I nodded. "Some show, huh?"

Parroting the Ray Stevens' song, Walter said, "I hollered, 'Don't look, Dilly! But it was too late. She'd done been mooned.'"

We all laughed—except Dilly, who merely rolled her eyes.

"I hope they caught that imbecile last night," she said. "He's ruining the fair. Would you want to take your kids there knowing they're liable to see that?"

"I don't want to take myself there knowing I'm liable to see that again," I said. "The only reason I went last night was—" I faltered, not wanting to tell them the full reason I was there. "—was because Sawyer Sykes is an old friend of my mom's."

"Really?" Dilly asked. "That's exciting."

"Not as much as you think. He's kind of a jerk."

"Well, if he had anything to do with that streaker, I'm inclined to agree," Walter said.

"Why do you think he had something to do with the streaker?" Jackie asked.

"Because when the streaker came out, the band began playing that old song, *The Streak*." I got the coffee pot containing French vanilla and poured both Dilly and Walter a cup. "That seemed suspicious to me too, Walter. And one of the police officers overseeing the fair had the same thought we did."

"Do they think the band hired the streaker or something?" Scott asked, bringing plates and the cake knife from the kitchen.

"I don't know," I said. "I believe the main thing the police want to know is whether the streaker had anything to do with Mabel Hobbs' murder. After all, he provided the commotion necessary to kill the woman in a large crowd of people without anyone—with the possible exception of Maude Ennis—seeing what happened."

"Maude Ennis is full of hot air," Jackie said. "Granny would never have hit Mabel over the head with that jar of pickles."

"How is Aunt Bess?" Luis asked. "Is she scared? I'd be afraid of getting blamed for something I didn't do."

I imagined Aunt Bess was terrified, but I didn't want to say so, especially in front of Jackie. "She knows the police are determined to find out who really killed Mabel. Aunt Bess is a pillar of the community—they're convinced she's innocent. They simply have to find the proof."

"Let's dig into this cake," Scott said.

Later, after the morning rush, I called Daphne Jacobs and made an appointment to meet with the baker at her home in Brea Ridge. The café closed at three o'clock, so I arranged to meet with Daphne at three-thirty.

I thought about calling Mom and asking her what the deal was between her and Sawyer, but I didn't want to get aggravated so early in the day. My best bet would be to try to put Sawyer out of my mind until this evening.

Upon leaving the kitchen, I saw Homer approaching the counter. "Good morning. Who's your hero today?"

"Hermann Hesse, the poet," Homer said. "Hesse once said, 'Everything becomes a little different as soon as it is spoken out loud.'"

"I get that," I said. "And you've batted home the agreement I made with myself before I left the kitchen— don't have a conversation I know won't end well so early in the day."

"This conversation isn't with me, I hope."

"No, Homer, you're a dear. Other people..." I shook my head. "Not so much."

"Would you like to talk about it?" he asked.

"Not really. Suffice it to say my mother is acting like a child." I got him a cup of coffee. "I'll have your sausage biscuit ready in a few minutes."

"Take your time, and Amy?"

"Yes?"

"Remember your teen years—how much you resented it when your mother treated you as if you were behaving childishly?" He smiled slightly. "It made no difference whether you were or not, the fact remained that you wanted to live your own life and make your own choices."

Pressing my lips together momentarily, I said, "Yeah, but this is different."

"Is it? 'Some of us think holding on makes us strong; but sometimes it is letting go.' Hesse."

"Smart guy." That's what I said. What I was thinking was wonder how Hesse would feel if Sawyer Sykes was trying to worm his way back into *his* mother's life?

It was near closing time, the café was empty, and I was deciding between chicken Parmesan and stuffed bell peppers for tomorrow's special when Sawyer sauntered into the café.

"Well, well, well." He smirked at me. "I had to see this for myself. Jenna told me little Amy was all grown up and running her own restaurant."

"Hello, Sawyer."

He spread his arms. "You got a hug for your old Uncle Saw?"

Jackie, who'd been rolling out pie crusts, burst out of the kitchen. "Nobody here has anything for you other than a kick in the butt if you don't hit the road."

Scott and Luis closed ranks as well, although Jackie was by far the most intimidating.

"Jackie Fonseca, fiery as ever." Sawyer chuckled.

"Won't you have a seat and a cup of coffee?" I asked.

"Amy—"

I interrupted my cousin with an arched eyebrow. She knew me well enough to know I had my reasons.

"All right." She nodded. "I'll get back to my pie crusts. Give a shout if you need me."

Scott and Luis followed suit and resumed their tasks.

"So, how've you been?" I poured the last of the French vanilla into a cup and placed it in front of him, not really caring if he'd like the flavored coffee or not. I wasn't conducting a sweet reunion—this was an interrogation.

"Been doing well." He looked around at the café. "Appears you have been too."

I had so much I wanted to say to this man. *Are you trying to worm your way back into my mom's life* for starters. But Homer had been right about Mom being an adult, and there was more at stake here than Mom setting herself up to get hurt again. Aunt Bess could actually go to prison.

"Are you responsible for the streaker at the fair?" I asked.

He laughed. "Of everything I contemplated you saying to me, that never once crossed my mind."

Shrugging, I said, "And yet that's all I really want to know."

"Why's that?"

"Mom didn't tell you Aunt Bess is being questioned about a murder that took place on Monday while the crowd was distracted by your streaker?"

Sawyer raised his hands. "Hey, I never said he was my streaker. And, for what it's worth, I'm sorry your great-aunt got caught up in a bad situation."

"How do you explain playing the guy's theme music when he showed up last night if he isn't your streaker?" I asked. "Coincidence?"

"Opportunity. After the performance he gave on Monday night—and got away with it—I thought he might put in another appearance. The band and I worked on that song for hours to prepare in case he should show himself again. Pun intended."

"That's a lot of work to do on a hunch."

"It paid off." He grinned. "Didn't it?"

"I guess it did. So when and where is your next gig?"

"We don't have another one for two weeks," he said. "The band is taking a well-earned vacation, and I believe I'll hang around Winter Garden for a little while." Nodding toward the coffee he hadn't touched, he asked, "What do I owe you?"

"It's on the house." I'd been getting ready to throw it out and wash the pot anyway, but I kept that part to myself.

"Well, thank you kindly." He stood. "I'll try to get back by here and visit with you again before I leave town."

Yippee.

Gayle Leeson

Chapter Six

On the drive to Daphne Jacobs' house, I thought about the relationship I'd once had with Sawyer Sykes. Sure, he'd been Mom's boyfriend, but he'd been the closest thing I'd had to a dad since I was four and my own dad walked out of our lives for good.

I sighed. Mom and I had both loved Sawyer. He'd take me to the parking lot of the abandoned grocery store and let me drive his old pickup truck. The three of us would watch scary movies together on Friday nights. I always held the popcorn, and he always made me jump and spill it. Mom acted angry that we'd gotten popcorn all over the living room, but she hadn't really minded. It was fun. We were a family.

Until we weren't.

Until Sawyer got the call from a friend in Nashville who was starting up a new band.

Until he made excuses as to why we couldn't join him.

Until he dumped us.

And now he's back. What does he want?

I wasn't convinced he and his band weren't behind the whole streaker debacle. And if they were responsible for that, then they might even be accountable—however indirectly—for Mabel Hobbs' murder.

Daphne's house smelled like vanilla and coconut. The baker, who worked out of her home, ushered me into the living room and asked if I'd like something to drink. I declined and noticed the collection of framed photographs on the mantel: Daphne with the famed cake decorator Kerry Vincent; Daphne and her husband on their wedding day; an adorable baby; that same child through the years; a graduation photo of a young woman and man who looked very much alike—the twins, Daphne's niece and nephew. I recognized Leslie from the photo Scott had shown us this morning.

"What a beautiful family," I said. "I appreciate your taking time out of your busy day to see me."

Smiling, she said, "Happy to do it. There's a cake in the oven and some cupcakes are cooling, so I have a few minutes. Besides, I'm always delighted to talk with a fellow entrepreneur, especially one in the food industry. What can I do for you, Amy?"

"I saw your display at the fair earlier this week—it's gorgeous, by the way—and I wanted to ask what guidelines you were given with regard to judging the cake entries."

"Um, I wasn't really given any guidelines, per se. The coordinators simply asked me how I'd be scoring the entries. I told them I'd be judging them on level of skill—beginner, advanced, and child, since children ten and under had their own category—presentation, originality, creativity, design, level of difficulty, and number of decorating techniques used."

I nodded. "I can't imagine anyone would think themselves more qualified to judge a cake decorating competition than Brea Ridge's own award-winning decorator. It appears you held the contestants to a high standard."

"I did. High but fair." Daphne frowned slightly. "Is that why you're here? Did you or someone you know enter a cake that you believe was judged too harshly?"

"Goodness, no! In fact, the cake competition was the only one at the fair that my friend Sarah and I felt confident was impartially judged." I explained to Daphne about some of the other exhibits we'd seen. "And take the biscuits. I know biscuits. And maybe the blue-ribbon winners tasted way better than the others, but those didn't look like first-place biscuits to me."

"I agree," she said. "I saw those biscuits—flatter than a flitter, as my grandmother used to say. And I didn't look at all of the exhibits, but I thought some of the winners fell short of hitting the mark set by the second- and third-place entrants." She shrugged. "I chalked it up to the subjectiveness of art. I'm sure some people would have judged the cake decorating entries differently from the way I did, and I imagine that not everybody was happy with my decisions."

"I know. And, really, I didn't think anything of it when Aunt Bess said Mabel Hobbs had been cheating by using store-bought pickles to enter the competition—I figured it was sour grapes on Aunt Bess's part—until Sarah and I looked around and saw some of those winners that made us think they were chosen by someone putting all the contestants' names on a dart board, closing their eyes, and then throwing a dart to choose a winner." I sighed. "Mainly, I'm looking for a reason that Mabel Hobbs was murdered."

"I heard about that," Daphne said. "Your Aunt Bess—is she the woman—?"

"The woman who was standing beside Mabel? The woman who'd been arguing with the victim moments before she was bashed over the head with a jar of prize-winning pickles? Yep, that's Aunt Bess."

"Oh, man." She leaned back in her chair. "And you know she's innocent. No wonder you're looking anywhere and everywhere for answers."

"I knew you'd understand."

"Let's say the judges did choose the winner using some criteria other than best entry," Daphne said. "What would they gain by it? Would anyone actually bribe a county-fair judge to give him or her the blue ribbon for cornbread? That doesn't make any sense."

"No, it doesn't," I said. "What's to be gained other than bragging rights? Plus, I thought these were blind entries."

"They were." She lifted her face toward the ceiling. "Of course, you could tell a judge, 'Mine is the photograph of the lightning strike over a lake' or something like that. Sorry, I remembered that photo because it was stunning."

"I remember that one too. It didn't win anything."

She looked at me. "Are you kidding?"

I shook my head. "Not even an honorable mention. Do you think it could be possible that the judges scoring certain events were biased against the best entries and believed they were doing the other entrants a kindness by allowing them to win? You know, something along the lines of 'Poor old Maude Crabtree enters her horrible biscuits in this competition every year, and she's just turned a million and four, so let's throw her a bone.'"

"It's certainly possible. Unjust to the people with the superior entries, but possible." She blew out a breath. "I'm kind of upset that the lake photo didn't win anything. But, of course, that's not helping us solve your problem. Even if there was cheating on the part of the judges, I doubt seriously that Mabel Hobbs was killed because her pickles won first prize."

"Neither do I, but it's what the police think that matters."

"You know your great-aunt is innocent, or you wouldn't be investigating. Who else was at the scene of the crime—or who stood out among the horde of people at the fair?" she asked. "Do you even know?"

When I rattled off the list of suspects, Daphne smiled.

"I knew you were a kindred spirit," she said.

"I keep coming back to the streaker," I said. "While he obviously didn't commit the murder, I can't help but wonder if the killer set up the distraction."

She squinted at me. "I want to know why Mabel had to die then. Why did she have to die that night, at the fair, in the midst of a crowd of potential witnesses? What was so urgent it made the killer take such an astronomical risk?"

"You're right. Did the killer not know where Mabel lived? I find that hard to believe, especially in a town as small as Winter Garden—especially if the killer hated her enough to kill her and it wasn't a random act."

"Find out why the killer felt forced to behave so recklessly, and everything else will fall into place."

I was lighting two blue taper candles when I heard Ryan's sports car pull into the driveway. I texted him to come on into the kitchen, afraid that Princess Eloise would hop onto the table to investigate and set the house on fire if I turned my back on the curious cat.

"Hello," Ryan called as he walked into the house.

Both Rory and Princess Eloise ran to welcome him. Rory, I understood—the little brown terrier loved everyone he met. But Princess Eloise? Until Ryan came along, she loved Mom and tolerated everyone else, including me. Mom was still her number one, but Ryan was a close second.

Ryan came into the kitchen and greeted me with a kiss. He was special—there was no denying that. I couldn't blame the persnickety white Persian for falling for him too.

Drawing back to look at my face, Ryan said, "I could stare into those beautiful eyes of yours for hours."

I grinned. "If you did, your lasagna would get cold."

"Good thing I can eat and look at you at the same time. Anything I can do to help?"

"Nope. Everything is ready."

He pulled out my chair. "Have you had a good day?"

"I have," I said, as I took my seat. "I went to see Daphne Jacobs after work to ask her about the judging criteria given her by the fair coordinators. It was apparent to Sarah and me that the judges didn't score the entrants as we would have."

"And what did Daphne say?" He sat opposite me and took a sip of his iced tea.

"The coordinator trusted her to use her own criteria to choose her winners." I served Ryan a slice of lasagna before placing a square of it on my plate. "Daphne and I agreed that cheating judges or winning a pickle competition are unlikely motives for murder, but the real question is why was Mabel killed at the fair that night? Couldn't the murderer have waited for a more convenient time and place?"

"You'd think," he said.

"What about the streaker?" I asked.

"We still haven't been able to find him."

"How is a man that big and that naked so hard to pin down?"

Not ten minutes after Ryan left my house, Mom rapped on the back door. She must've been watching for him to leave.

Unlocking the door, I let her in, wary as to why she'd decided to visit so late. "Is anything wrong?"

"No." She pulled a chair out from the table and sat. "I merely wondered if Ryan mentioned anything about the Mabel Hobbs case while he was here."

I remained standing, hoping to convey that I was in no mood for an extended visit. "You know Ryan isn't allowed to discuss ongoing cases with me or anyone else not involved in the investigation."

"You *are* involved—we *all* are! Aunt Bess is either a suspect or a witness."

Hearing Mom's voice, Princess Eloise raced into the kitchen and hopped onto Mom's lap. Rory trotted along behind her with a green ball in his mouth.

Mom picked up Princess Eloise and nuzzled the cat's fluffy white head before tossing the ball for Rory.

"We both know you didn't come down here to talk about Mabel Hobbs," I said. "I take it you already know that Sawyer showed up at the café today."

"I wasn't aware he'd planned to visit you, but I'm not surprised. How did that go?"

Giving her an exaggerated blink, I asked, "How do you think it went? Jackie was ready to throttle him on sight. So was I, come to think of it, but I managed to control myself."

"Why would Jackie want to harm Sawyer?" she asked. "She barely knew the man."

"No, but she saw how hurt we both were when he left." I fought back tears. "You're not the only one he dumped, you know."

"I realize that. Why do you think I never dated anyone else until you were grown?"

"Does Clark know where you were last night?"

She raised her chin. "Yes."

"How did he feel about your walk down memory lane with Sawyer?"

"None of your business." She kissed Princess Eloise, gently placed the cat onto the floor, and left.

Rory came back after having retrieved the ball to find his playmate gone and me in tears. He spat out the ball, stood on his hindlegs, and licked my knee.

I bent and picked him up. "I adore you. There's nothing complicated about *our* relationship."

Chapter Seven

S cott was at the café when I got there the next morning. I checked my watch to make sure I wasn't late. I wasn't. In fact, I was early.

I hurried into the kitchen to find him cutting a roll of sausage into patties.

"Hey," I said. "Is anything wrong?"

"No." He placed the patties onto a sheet of waxed paper. "I wanted to talk to you before anyone else arrived."

"Oh, no." I groaned. "You aren't leaving me, are you?"

Jackie was already taking classes at the community college and planned to leave the café after earning her degree. And, although it was selfish of me, I hated the thought of losing Scott too.

"I'm not going anywhere, Amy-girl."

"Thank goodness for that."

"But what I'm about to tell you has to stay between us or else Ivy could get into trouble."

Scott's sister, Ivy, was Winter Garden's forensic specialist.

"I won't say a word to anyone," I said. "I promise."

"I was at her house last night, and her laptop was open. When I glanced at the screen, I saw that she'd been working in the Mabel Hobbs' file."

"And?" My mouth had gone dry, and my voice emerged as little more than a squeak.

"Mr. Hobbs must've been, like, super rich. He had his estate set up to where his wife could make use of his assets until her death. When she died, everything went to his children."

"That makes sense." I didn't understand why that was such a secret. I imagined that arrangement was common knowledge among the Hobbs' family at the very least.

"But here's the thing—Mabel was getting ready to pull a fast one on the heirs. Ivy found a check for half a mil on a desk in the Hobbs' den. It was dated for the day after she was killed, and it was made out to the fair committee."

Placing a hand on his arm, I said, "So Mabel's step-children had five-hundred-thousand reasons to want her dead before that check was handed over."

"Yep."

"And they, along with Bella's husband, were at the fair."

"Yep. And they know there are security cameras at the house, so they wouldn't have wanted to show up there," he said.

I released a breath. "This means Aunt Bess is in the clear."

"I wish it did, Amy-girl. But we've still got nada."

"Except a motive," I said. "We've got an excellent motive."

Sarah strolled into the café at around eight o'clock. She was wearing navy shorts, a coral tank top, and leather thong sandals—not her typical workday attire.

"Hi. Are you off work today?" I asked, already pouring her a cup of French vanilla coffee.

"Nope. Billy is. He and his family are on vacation."

"That's nice." I placed her coffee in front of her as she took a seat at the counter.

"It *is* nice—for both of us. Basically, all I'm doing is answering the phone." She sipped her coffee. "And sleuthing."

"Sleuthing?" I flattened my hand against my chest. "Do tell."

Jackie brought an order up to the front, saw that I was talking with Sarah, and went on into the kitchen. I was grateful she was giving me a breather. Traffic had slowed, but we'd had a busy morning so far.

"Yesterday, I kept wondering who'd want Mabel Hobbs dead. I mean, she seemed nice enough as far as I knew." She lowered her voice to a whisper, and I could barely hear her. "Did she harbor deep, dark secrets? Was it a crime of passion? Or was she killed purely for financial gain?"

"Would you like to take your coffee out to the patio? It would be quieter there." There was no one using the patio this morning. Most of our customers didn't venture out there until the brunch or lunch hours.

She nodded and slid off the stool.

As we passed by Scott, I asked him to give me a yell if he and Jackie needed me.

Sitting in a quiet corner of the patio, Sarah told me she'd spent the day yesterday going through the file on Mr. Hobbs' estate.

"Did you find anything that could be considered a motive for his wife's murder?" I asked.

"Possibly. Prior to his death, Mr. Hobbs paid five-thousand-dollars a month to a Zelda F. Gerald."

I raised my brows. "Zelda F. Gerald? Oh, that doesn't sound like an alias at all."

"Yeah, I also thought it was a little too cute. I mean, what are the odds a real person would have the same name as F. Scott Fitgerald's wife? Not impossible, but not likely, right? So, I did a search but couldn't find any *Zelda* who'd been a part of Mr. Hobbs' life." She shrugged. "I plan to keep digging today."

"The estate wasn't instructed to continue paying Zelda after Hobbs' death?"

"No, which has me thinking mistress. He'd have made a provision in his will had this woman been a relative."

"And a blackmailer would have been paid secretly and wouldn't have been on the books at all," I said.

"You'd think so. Then again, I'd have thought a mistress would have been paid on the down-low too." She took a drink of her coffee, wrinkled her nose, and pushed her cup away.

"Cold?"

"Tepid," she said.

"Sorry. Let me get you another cup."

"Make it to go please and give me one of those blueberry crullers I saw in the case. I need to get to the office."

"You've got it." I hopped up from the table. "Thanks for the intel."

"No problem. I just hope we can find our mystery lady." She stood. "I don't know if Zelda cared whether or not Mabel Hobbs lived or died, but things likely got tough for her when that monthly allowance stopped rolling in."

As Sarah was going out the door, a tour bus was rolling onto our parking lot. The bus was filled with tourists passing through on their way to Biltmore in Asheville, North Carolina. Normally, tour groups called to give us a heads-up that they were on their way. This one did not.

It was all hands on deck as Jackie, Luis, Scott, and I bustled around filling orders and trying to give one ornery trio a "Downton Abbey-ish experience." For us, that basically meant we served them tea instead of coffee. Had we been given some notice, I'd have been happy to make some scones, but there simply wasn't time to accommodate the wannabe Crawleys and the rest of the group as well.

Homer came in for his sausage biscuit at ten-thirty. The bus crowd was finishing up, so he didn't get to announce his hero of the day until after they'd left. By that time, Jackie's curiosity about my conversation with Sarah was driving her up the wall.

"Did Sarah find out anything new about Mabel Hobbs and who might've wanted her dead?" she asked, as I was pouring Homer's second cup of coffee.

Since Homer was practically family, none of us avoided speaking openly in front of him.

"There was a woman named Zelda—or using that name—who was being paid a hefty monthly allowance until Mr. Hobbs died," I said. "The estate wasn't instructed to continue paying her after his death."

"Who was she?" Jackie asked.

"I don't know. Sarah is going to try to find out more about her today."

"My hero of the day is the renowned coach, John Wooden, who once said, 'It's what you learn after you know it all that counts.' I realize Coach Wooden wasn't talking about criminal cases and evidence." Homer shrugged. "But I still think it could apply."

"I agree," I said.

"Me, too." Jackie drummed her fingertips on the counter. "I know Mr. Hobbs' son, Drew—we had a college class together. He was having to take an ethics class for continuing education. Anyway, I'll reach out to him to see what he might know about this Zelda. I saw on social media that the family is receiving guests wanting to pay their respects at the home this evening."

Realizing Jackie could be about as subtle as an orangutan with a sledgehammer, I volunteered to go with her.

Sarah had called after work to report that she'd been unable to discover any further information about Zelda F. Gerald. I'd told her that Jackie and I intended to visit the Hobbs' home later with some food, and she offered to tag along.

Now the three of us were standing on the front steps of a Georgian-style mansion with our casserole, brownies, and ham rolls.

An older lady—a friend of Mabel's, I assumed—greeted us at the door and asked us to sign a guestbook.

We sat the food on a table and signed the book, and I complimented the lady on her suit, a powder blue silk that really was gorgeous.

"Thank you." She smiled.

"Your name isn't Zelda, is it?" Jackie asked.

"No, dear. I'm June."

"Is Zelda here?" Sarah asked.

"Do you know Zelda?" Jackie's question tumbled out over Sarah's.

I felt sorry for the poor woman, who was looking really confused at this point. "Forgive my friends. They were really hoping to meet Ms. Gerald."

Drawing her brows together, she asked, "Who's Zelda Gerald? I've known Mabel for forty years and have never heard her mention anyone named Zelda."

Glancing at Sarah and Jackie proved futile. Neither of them was willing to help me explain to this lady who Zelda might be.

"I...um...Zelda might...I think she was..." I was struggling. "Mabel's babysitter."

"Mabel didn't have children," the woman said.

"Right," I said. "I was thinking Zelda was *Mabel's* babysitter." Worst. Liar. Ever.

"Well, honey, wouldn't a woman old enough to have cared for Mabel when she was a little girl be dead by now?" the woman asked.

Before I could answer, Jackie took me by the arm and dragged me into the living room where the rest of the so-called mourners had gathered. I used the term loosely because no one seemed sad, other than the woman manning the door.

Drew Hobbs was standing just inside the living room.

"Hi, Drew," Jackie said. "We brought some food. It's on a table in the foyer, but we'd be happy to put it in the kitchen."

"We'll get it," he said. "Thanks, Jackie. Nice of you to come."

Nobody mentioned the elephant in the room—that Jackie's grandmother was a suspect in his stepmother's murder.

Sarah and I expressed our condolences for his loss.

"Thanks, but I wasn't terribly close to my stepmother. I mean, she was nice enough, I guess; but if Dad was going to take the plunge and remarry, he could've done better."

"Didn't he date a woman named Zelda at some point?" Sarah asked.

"It's hard to say," Drew said. "Dad dated several women after Mom died, but he always said he was afraid they were after him for his money. Still, I wish he'd have chosen a more attractive gold-digger with a sweeter disposition."

He laughed, and the three of us forced a chuckle.

Bella, his sister, overheard what he'd said and joined our conversation. "I don't think Dad should have remarried at all after Mom died. I know he was lonely, but he had us and all his grandchildren. Why did he feel like he needed more family?"

"I disagree," Drew said. "The old guy needed someone here to keep him company and to take care of him. I just would have preferred someone other than Mabel."

"At least, we loved Dad," Bella said. "I'm not sure Mabel ever did."

"I was asking your brother if you remembered your dad dating someone named Zelda," Sarah said.

"Zelda?" Bella shook her head. "That name doesn't ring any bells for me."

Unfortunately, Mabel's friend in the powder blue suit, stepped into the living room and heard part of our conversation.

Pencil-thin eyebrows raised, she asked, "You think Ralph dated Mabel's *babysitter*?"

I took in the expressions of bewilderment on the siblings' faces and screwed my face into a look similar to theirs. "If you'll excuse me, I need to go get that casserole and put it into the refrigerator."

Feeling no shame in leaving Jackie and Sarah to clean up their own mess, I scooted back to the foyer, grabbed the casserole dish and the platter of ham rolls and took them into the kitchen. There I found Mark, Bella's husband, who was having a glass of wine. As soon as he began to speak, I realized it wasn't his first.

"Hello," he said. "You're the gal who runs the Down South Café, right?"

"I am." I nodded toward the refrigerator. "Do you think there's room in there for these?"

"We'll make room, darlin'." He opened the door. "I've been meaning to stop by and check out your place. I hear good things about it all the time."

"Thank you." I wedged the casserole dish into the refrigerator and then placed the platter of ham rolls on top of it.

"I'm glad you came by. It took some nerve on your part, didn't it? I mean, what with your aunt being accused of whacking Mabel over the head with that pickle jar and all."

"I'm sure my great-aunt had nothing to do with your stepmother's death."

"Fffttt." He flung a hand toward me. "Don't worry about it. If she *had* brained the old gal, she'd have been doing us all a favor. That woman *hated* us. She was always doing things to spite us."

"She was?" I asked. "Like what?"

"Well, she was getting ready to throw a big chunk of our inheritance away to some charity I doubt she even cared about. She didn't want us to have it, that's all there was to it."

"But I thought Mr. Hobbs was also a philanthropist," I said. "Wasn't there an organization headed up by Zelda Gerald that he made generous donations to?"

"I don't know anything about that, but you're right that Ralph gave plenty of money away. And more power to him. It was *his* money. Mabel had no right to blow his money simply because it was going to become *our* money upon her death, and she wanted to keep us from getting it."

"Well." I took a backward step toward the door. "I hope you enjoy the food."

"Me, too. Thanks again."

Maude Ennis walked into the kitchen with a platter filled with flat, dry-looking biscuits. Her attention focused on Mark, she said, "I've brought you some of my blue-ribbon-winning biscuits!"

"What a joy." His voice was drier than her biscuits.

Turning around and recognizing me, Maude said, "No wonder Mark is in such a foul mood. The great-niece of the woman who killed his stepmother is here. May I ask what makes you so brazen as to show up to my dear friend's memorial?"

Mark took it upon himself to answer on my behalf. "She brought us some *good* food, Maude. But I'm sure your shotputs will be appreciated too. Maybe we can get in some target practice in the morning."

On our way back to the café where Jackie and Sarah had left their cars, I told them about my encounters with Mark and Maude.

"I don't think anyone I spoke with has a clue who Zelda is or was to Mr. Hobbs," I said. "But none of the heirs is broken up about Mabel's death, and they all had a motive to kill her before she completely depleted their inheritance."

Chapter Eight

After visiting the Hobbs' house, Sarah, Jackie, and I needed a pick-me-up. We'd taken my car, so rather than return to the café where we'd met, I drove us to an ice cream parlor in Brea Ridge. On the way, Jackie texted Roger and Ryan and asked them to meet us there. Unfortunately, John was back at school.

The guys arrived at the ice cream shop before we did, and they got us a table.

"How was your visit to the bereaved?" Roger asked, as we were sitting down.

"Well, they weren't very bereaved," Jackie said.

"That's for sure." I blew out a breath. "I didn't know Mabel personally, but I feel sorry for her now."

Ryan stood. "I'll put in our orders. What does everyone want?"

Sarah and I ordered caramel sundaes with peanuts; Jackie ordered a banana split, which Roger said he'd share with her; and Ryan ordered a hot fudge sundae.

The ice cream parlor wasn't crowded this late on a Thursday evening, so the rowdy bunch of teens bursting through the door didn't go unnoticed.

"That's William Fairley," Sarah whispered to me, nodding to the boy leading the charge. He had dark auburn hair and was wearing a black t-shirt with the sleeves cut off.

"Isn't he the one Mabel had accused of stealing t-shirts at the fair?" I asked.

"Yes," Ryan said, returning to the table in time to hear my question. "And he's no stranger to law enforcement. He's been involved in a lot of petty juvenile stuff—but he turned eighteen last week."

"So his prior slaps on the wrist will be more serious punishments going forward," Roger said.

"Exactly. Unless he turns himself around." Ryan shook his head. "I hope he will. I hate to see a kid throw his future away."

"Did the police speak to him about Mabel's murder?" I asked quietly.

"The sheriff did," Ryan said. "Naturally, the kid denied everything, including stealing the shirts, and there were people who said they saw him in another area of the building when Mabel was struck down."

"Huh." I stood. "Will Fairley?"

"What are you doing?"

"Amy—"

"Are you sure—?"

Ignoring the protests of my friends, I remained standing.

Will Fairley pointed to himself. "Me?"

I nodded. "May I speak with you for a second?"

He shrugged and strode toward our table, looking back over his shoulder at his buddies who were snickering as they watched.

"What do you want?" he asked. "A date?"

Pushing an empty chair toward him, I asked him to take a seat as I returned to my own. "It'll only take a minute."

Glancing back at his friends, he shrugged again before sitting on the chair. "Be quick. I'm holding up my buds."

"My great-aunt was standing beside Mabel Hobbs on Monday night when Mabel was hit with the pickle jar," I said.

Will held up his hands in protest. "I didn't have anything to do with that."

"I'm not saying you did. I'm merely asking for your help." I waited until he met my eyes. "Someone has come forward and accused my aunt of hitting Mabel. I know she's innocent, and I'm asking everyone I know of who was at the fair if they saw anything that might help her. You were at the fair on Monday, weren't you?"

"Yeah, I was there." He pushed an unruly lock of hair off his forehead. "All I know is that people started clustering around and running in all directions when that fat, naked guy plowed through the crowd."

"Totally." A girl from Will's group inched closer to put in her two cents. "We were all afraid he'd touch us or something. I mean, gross! What kind of perv takes off his clothes and runs through a public place?"

"The kind of perv who'll do anything if the price is right," Will said. "I told you that, Cami."

"Wait," Ryan said. "What makes you think somebody paid him?"

"I saw them. I was over at the t-shirt—" Will broke off, realizing he was about to incriminate himself.

"Nobody cares about any t-shirts," Ryan said. "A woman was murdered, and if you're right that the streaker was paid to provide a distraction, then the person who paid him might be the killer."

"Can't help you there. The guy who paid the big guy had his back to me," Will said.

"How do you know the man who had his back to you was paying the other one to run naked through the fairgrounds?" Jackie asked.

"Because the big guy had on bibbed overalls and a t-shirt; and as soon as he got his money, he started taking off his clothes."

"Did you tell any of this to the sheriff?" Ryan asked.

Will lifted and dropped one shoulder. "Guess I forgot."

"Thank you for telling us," I said before Ryan could berate Will for not being more forthcoming before.

"The man was wearing bibs," Sarah said. "You think he might've been a farmer?"

"Jeremy did say he saw the guy at the Angus exhibit earlier that evening," the girl Will had called Cami said.

"The police have asked every vendor at the fair if they saw anything." Ryan ran a hand through his hair. "No one seemed to know anything about the streaker."

"They don't want to talk to the cops," Will said. "Nobody wants to wind up on a witness stand." He jerked his chin toward Jackie, Sarah, and me. "You need to send your undercover babes. I bet they could get some answers."

"He's right," I said. "Nobody wants to put themselves in a position to have to testify against someone, especially if they think he was simply pulling a prank that had nothing to do with Mabel Hobbs' murder. We need a new plan." I smiled at Will.

Will gulped and looked at Ryan. "I don't like how she's looking at me."

"Neither do I," Ryan said. "That expression usually means she has a really bad idea."

I actually had a good idea that I explained to everyone—including Will and all his friends—over ice cream, which I bought because bribes sometimes worked. And I needed all the help I could get.

On Friday morning, Dilly and Walter were the café's first customers, as usual.

Walter greeted Scott with a clap on the back. "Scott, have you asked that young lady out on a date yet?"

"Not yet, Walter. I need to get to know her a little better first."

"Bah!" Walter flung a hand dismissively. "What better way to get to know someone than over a meal?"

"I know, I know." Scott grinned. "I'm just not as smooth as you, man."

Dilly sat down and, since the café was empty as far as other customers went, called out her order. "I'd like crepes with fresh strawberries this morning. And don't forget Buddy's biscuit!"

"I'm on it," I said.

"I'd like an omelet please." Walter sat across from his wife. "Lots of cheese and bacon."

"You've got it." I went into the kitchen to get started on their meals.

Jackie followed me and started working on the omelet as I mixed up the batter for the crepes. "Do you really think those little juvenile delinquents will do a good job of finding out who hired the streaker?"

"They'll come closer to finding out than any of the rest of us have," I said. "Besides, Roger will be there playing chaperone."

"Yeah, I'm not so sure he was delighted that you volunteered him for that job."

I grinned. "He'll be good for them. I'll bet you a coconut cake to your banana pudding that Roger has Will working for him before the evening is over."

"You're on. And I'm going to enjoy every bite of that coconut cake."

"I can almost taste that banana pudding now." I licked my lips. "Yum, yum, yum."

Scott poked his head into the kitchen. "There's a woman named Bella here to see you."

"Go," Jackie said. "I can finish up here."

Bella was sitting at the counter in a black maxi dress. She wore silver jewelry, and her hair was loose and wavy. "Good morning."

"Hi, Bella. Would you like some coffee?"

"Yes, black, please."

"All right." I got the carafe of dark roast coffee and poured a cup for Bella. "Would you like something to eat?"

"No, thank you." She looked over her shoulder to where Dilly and Walter sat.

The older couple was pretending not to listen, but I knew them well enough to say for certain that they were.

Bella lowered her voice so much, I had to lean closer to hear. "I apologize for my husband's behavior last night. Mark had too much to drink and not enough to eat, and I'm afraid he might've said some inappropriate things about my stepmother." She sighed. "I mean, even though Mabel wasn't our favorite person, she was Dad's wife. He loved her."

"I understand," I said.

"Dad was an adult. I mean—" She fidgeted with her necklace. "I said things I shouldn't have said too. I didn't realize how I sounded until I heard how irrational Mark was being. I wished I'd come to my senses sooner and had treated Mabel like a member of the family. Maybe then Mabel wouldn't have felt compelled to try to undermine me and my brother every chance she got, and our dad would've been happier too."

"Don't think another thing about it." I smiled. "Tensions always run high at a time like this. It's to be expected."

As I went back into the kitchen to help Jackie, I made a mental note to call Mom later. Whatever she wanted to do with her life was her choice. I wouldn't want her dictating how she wanted me to live my life. I owed her the same respect.

"What did she want?" Jackie asked.

"I believe she was simply doing damage control because Mark was a little loose-lipped last night."

"They all were, if you want my opinion." She plated the omelet and put a strawberry rose on the plate.

"True, but that doesn't mean they killed Mabel," I said.

"Doesn't mean they're innocent either."

Chapter Nine

After work on Friday, Roger took Will and Cami to the fair. He wouldn't hear of allowing Jackie or me to pay their expenses—he said he had as much to gain as we did from keeping Aunt Bess out of prison. Besides, he'd reasoned, when would he get a better opportunity to be a role model to impressionable teens? Jackie had beamed with pride until—behind Roger's back—I pantomimed eating banana pudding.

While Roger and the teens were at the fair, Jackie and I went to the big house to visit Mom and Aunt Bess.

Aunt Bess was shouting an answer to a game show's question when Jackie and I arrived. She was wrong, and the contestant was too, having given the same answer as Aunt Bess.

Turning off the television, she shook her head in disgust, setting her white curls to bobbing. "That show cheats people sometimes. We were right—that girl and I. That game is rigged."

"Where's Mom?" I asked.

"She's in the kitchen, I believe." She peered behind us. "Where are those handsome fellas of yours?"

"Ryan had to work," I said.

"So did Roger."

I figured Jackie was only bending the truth a little bit. While Roger might not be working at his construction business, he was working on finding the streaker, who might be able to shed light on who'd killed Mabel Hobbs. And if Aunt Bess knew he was at the fair doing some detecting, we'd be hard pressed to keep her from joining him.

Mom was cubing some watermelon when I walked into the kitchen. "Need any help?" I asked.

"No, thanks." She didn't look up from her task.

"I'm sorry." I pulled out a chair and sat. "Your love life is none of my business, and I had no right to be upset about your going out with Sawyer."

"You're entitled to your opinion." She finally dragged her gaze to meet mine. "But last night, you didn't even give me an opportunity to explain."

"You don't owe me any explanations. I want you to do whatever makes you happy."

"Thanks. I will." Her mouth turned up on one side as she fought off a smile. "And FYI, I'm not leaving Clark for Sawyer. I only met with Sawyer to give him a piece of my mind."

I let out a breath I hadn't realized I'd been holding. "Oh, thank goodness."

Allowing herself that smile now, Mom said, "I'm still sort of ticked off at you. How dumb do you think I am?"

"I acknowledge your brilliance, but I also remember how much you cared about Sawyer."

"He had me fooled once. Now my eyes are wide open."

"I'm glad. I just want you to be happy, Mom."

"I know," she said. "And I am happy."

"What are you two doing in here?" Aunt Bess asked, as she and Jackie joined us. "You came in here thirty minutes ago to cut up that watermelon, Jenna. What's the hold up?"

Giving me a pointed look, Mom said, "Correction—I was."

"You were what?" Aunt Bess asked.

"Cutting up this watermelon, Aunt Bess." She rolled her eyes at me. "But I'm done now."

Jackie and I prepared an easy pasta dish for dinner; and then after helping Mom with the cleanup, we went down to my house. Aunt Bess was a little pouty that we weren't staying to watch TV with her, but Jackie promised to come back up before she went home.

"She'd love it if you moved in," I said, as we walked down the hill.

"And I'd hate it."

We both laughed as we went into the kitchen through the back door. I was immediately greeted by a wiggly Rory. Princess Eloise sauntered into the kitchen and imperiously waited to be noticed. Rory went from me to Jackie and back again.

"Hello, Princess Eloise," I said.

The Persian ignored me and daintily gave her left front paw a lick.

"Let me get these two fed, and then I'll whip up a batch of brownies for Roger and the kids to have when they get here."

"You take care of the pets," she said. "I'll work on the brownies. Consider them your consolation prize because you won't be getting that banana pudding."

I merely smiled and fed Rory and Princess Eloise.

Jackie had taken out the brownies only about five minutes before Roger, Will, and Cami arrived.

"Mm-mm, this house smells good!" Roger said, as he came through the front door followed by the teens.

"Jackie made brownies," I said. "They need to cool for a few minutes, and then you can help yourselves."

We went into the kitchen where Roger, Jackie, Will, and Cami sat at the table. I poured tea for everyone before sitting at the island. Rory was slightly unsure about the teenagers, so he lay by the door.

"Any luck finding the streaker?" Jackie asked.

Roger nodded at Will, who looked particularly pleased with himself when he said, "Malcolm Smith."

"How'd you find out?" I asked.

"Nothin' to it." He smiled broadly, his eyes lingering on Cami. "We already knew he was likely one of the Angus farmers, right?"

"Okay, but I doubt he was hanging around the booth knowing full well the police were after him," Jackie said.

"He wasn't," Will said, "at least, not out in the open. But a man doesn't abandon a herd of cattle that valuable."

"Will had the most amazing idea," Cami said. "He went to the taco vendor and got some ground beef, corn, and shredded lettuce. Then he bought a cup of chili from the hot dog stand and mixed it all up together."

"That sounds disgusting." I wrinkled my nose.

"It was, but I had to make it look nasty," Will said. "When no one was looking, I poured it right outside the cattle stall."

"He didn't want it to be close enough that the cows could actually eat it and get sick," Cami said. "I think that was sweet."

"Thanks." Will grinned at her before continuing his story. "So, after I'd poured it there onto the ground and hidden the cup, I yelled, 'Gross! This cow is throwing up!'"

"When he heard that, Malcolm Smith came out from behind a divider to check on his livestock," Roger said.

"You bet he did," Will said. "And I said, 'Hey, you're that streaker, aren't you?' But all he wanted to know was which cow was sick."

"That's when Ryan and I stepped forward, and Ryan told Mr. Smith he needed to take him to the station for questioning," Roger said. "He was still worried about the cattle until Will told him it was a joke."

"I almost felt sorry for him because he was so upset about his cows," Cami said. "But one of the other deputies promised to stay with them until Mr. Smith got back."

"So, Ryan is talking with the streaker right now?" I asked.

Roger nodded.

"We have plenty of brownies." I shrugged. "I *could* box some up, and we could take them to the police station."

"Are we all going?" Cami asked. "I've never seen the inside of a police station before."

"It's no big deal," Will said.

"Sure, we can all go," I said. "After all, we're making a social call." I took Roger's arm and led him out of earshot of our guests. "Did you offer Will a job?"

"No."

"Oh, I—"

"I mean, not *just* Will," he interrupted me. "He and Cami are both going to be working for me part-time while learning a trade at the community college. Will is interested in masonry, and Cami wants to try electricity."

Laughing, I patted his back. "That's fantastic."

"Thanks. I'm happy about it too."

Chapter Ten

Roger, Jackie, Will, and Cami piled into Roger's pickup truck. I took the brownies in my car because, despite the truck being a king cab, four people was all the truck would comfortably hold. We drove to the police station.

With it being later in the evening, most of the officers on duty were out patrolling so the station was practically deserted when we arrived. I got there first and heard voices coming from the back offices. When the rest of the group came inside, I held up a hand to signal them to be quiet but to follow me.

From the hallway, we heard an interrogation taking place. A man—I was guessing Malcolm Smith, the streaker—was saying, "It was a lark...you know? The manager for one of the bands put me up to it, said it would be funny and that it would drum up interest in the fair."

"And you went along with it?" Sheriff Billings asked. "Just like that?"

"Well, I—" The man cleared his throat. "I was always known in school as the guy who'd do anything for a laugh. Class clown and all. I reckon I thought I could relive some of my glory days, you know?"

"Glory days." The words fell flat as they left the sheriff's lips. "You took off your clothes and ran naked through a crowd of people in order to relive your glory days."

"Well, that, and he paid me."

"He paid you." Ryan was chiming in now.

"Uh-huh."

"Why do you think he'd pay you to streak at the fair?" Ryan asked.

"Like I said, he told me it'd drum up business. They had a song about it and everything."

Sheriff Billings clucked his tongue. "Let me make sure I'm understanding this correctly. In order to relive your glory days and make a few bucks, you took off your clothes and ran through the exhibit hall of the county fair."

"Well, uh, yeah," the man said. "It sounds stupid when you say it like that."

"Sounds stupid?" Ryan asked. "How do you think it looked?"

"Let's set aside your actions for the moment, Mr. Smith, and talk about Mabel Hobbs. Surely, you're aware that a woman was murdered while you were running through the exhibit hall in your birthday suit."

"Yes, sir, I'm aware of that, and I'm sorry. But I didn't have anything to do with her."

"Yet you knew the police were looking for you," Ryan said. "Why didn't you come forward?"

"Because I was afraid," Mr. Smith said. "I didn't want you to think I had anything to do with killing Mabel. In fact, that's why I agreed to streak again the next night—to prove I didn't do anything but pull a harmless prank."

"There wasn't anything harmless about it," the sheriff said. "Even setting what happened to Mabel Hobbs aside, there were kids there, people running and afraid because they didn't know what you were doing. Your actions have consequences, Mr. Smith—legal consequences."

"I know. And I'm sorry."

"Still, I don't believe you had anything to do with Ms. Hobbs' murder," Sheriff Billings continued. "But to avoid an accessory to murder charge, I need to know the name of the man who hired you to streak."

"All I know is that his name was Harold, and he manages that Sykes feller," Mr. Smith said.

At that, Cami sneezed, and the gig was up.

I heard a chair scraping backward across the tile floor, and then Ryan came to the door.

"Hi!" I forced a smile. "We brought you and the sheriff some brownies."

"Thanks, but we're in the middle of an interrogation, and you need to leave." His voice was as firm as I'd ever heard it, but he did take the brownies. I thought that was a good sign that I'd be forgiven for eavesdropping.

Out in the parking lot, our little band of spies convened by Roger's truck to discuss what we'd heard.

"No one would pay a guy to streak through a crowd of people to provide a distraction so one old lady could be murdered," Jackie said.

"Unless he was a total psycho," Cami said.

"Why her?" I asked. "As we've already discussed, it would have been much easier and far less risky to have killed her somewhere else."

"Yeah," Roger said. "Why would Harold, the band manager, want to kill an old lady?"

"Part of me would love to blame this on Sawyer Sykes somehow," Jackie said, "but I can't come up with a motive for him to kill Mabel either."

"The motive," I said. "It all comes down to the motive."

When I got home, I called Sarah to get her opinion. After telling her about our serendipitous overhearing of part of Malcolm Smith's interrogation, I asked her if she thought it possible that Harold the band manager might be connected to Zelda, the mystery woman.

"Did Mr. Smith mention how old Harold was?" she asked. "Ralph Hobbs paid Zelda that monthly allowance for over four decades."

"He didn't say—at least, not while we were listening. You think Harold could be the child of Ralph and Zelda? That what—he was angry because Ralph had married Mabel after his first wife died instead of his mother?"

"Anything is possible, I guess."

I blew out a breath. "I don't get how Ralph could've kept an illegitimate child secret for all those years. Especially in Winter Garden. And, in particular, after Ralph died. I mean, wouldn't Harold have wanted his share of the inheritance?"

"You'd think," Sarah said. "Plus, if he was upset that Ralph hadn't married his mother, why would he wait until Ralph was dead and take out his anger on Mabel? What difference would it make after Ralph was dead? Ugh. I'm bad at this detecting stuff."

"No, you're not! We wouldn't even know about Zelda if not for you. None of this makes any sense—to anybody. If it did, we'd have our killer."

"I'll stop by the office in the morning and check the file for any mention of a Harold."

"It can wait until Monday," I said. "I'd hate—"

"It can't wait," she said. "It would drive me crazy all weekend if I didn't go in and have a look at the file."

"Thanks, Sarah."

"Anytime. I'll let you know what I find."

Once we'd disconnected, I stared down at the phone in my hand. I was thinking about Ryan. And brownies. And how I'd used those brownies for evil instead of good. I hadn't meant to, but that's how it had worked out.

I texted him: *I love you, and I'm sorry we eavesdropped on Mr. Smith's interrogation. It wasn't intentional, but I could've left or made my presence known, and I didn't. Please don't hold the brownies responsible for my actions.*

I saw the dots indicating Ryan was typing a response to my text.

I could no more expect the sun not to shine than you not to snoop. And Sheriff Billings and I both held the brownies harmless. So did Malcolm Smith, by the way.

I was kind of glad Malcolm Smith got a brownie too—him being the focus of the spy mission and all. I texted back that I'd make him a big breakfast tomorrow morning to make up for any trouble I'd caused him. He wrote back that he'd take me up on that.

As an afterthought, I added: *I don't think Mr. Smith was directly involved in Mabel Hobbs' murder, at least, from what I heard.*

I watched the dots for what seemed like a long time, and then I got this response. *See you in the morning.*

Was there something he wasn't telling me? Something pertinent to the investigation that he couldn't tell me? Was it about Mr. Smith's involvement? Or was it about Harold, Sawyer Sykes' band manager? I wondered what Sawyer might be willing to tell me about Harold?

The next morning, I went to work and immediately mixed up some pancake batter. I was planning to make Ryan pancakes, biscuits and gravy, eggs, and bacon...or sausage—his choice. Scott got to the café only minutes after I'd arrived, and I asked him to go ahead and start on the biscuits.

"What's up?" he asked. "Is there a tour bus coming?"

"Not that I know of." I explained about last night and how I owed Ryan an apology breakfast.

He grinned. "I'm sure you don't owe him anything, Amy-girl, but it's nice of you to make him a feast just the same."

Patting his shoulder, I said, "You deserve a feast. You're one in a million."

"Thanks. I hope Leslie will think so. I called her last night—to talk cake decorating techniques."

"Of course." I hid a smile. "How did it go?"

"We talked about cakes for a few minutes, but then we talked about everything else. When I looked at the clock, I saw that we'd been talking for over an hour."

"It went that well, huh? Wow."

He blushed before ducking his head. "I'd better see to the biscuits."

Luis came in and was greeting Scott and me when Sarah called. I slipped on my headset so I could speak with her while continuing to work.

"Did you find anything about Harold in Mr. Hobbs' estate file?" I asked.

"No. There wasn't any mention of a Malcolm Smith either. But get this—while I was looking through the file, Billy came in to go through the mail he'd received while he'd been away." She scoffed. "It wasn't like he didn't call every single day to see what was going on with his clients, but I guess he'd stayed away as long as he could."

"I understand," I said. "Take it from somebody who owns a business. Sometimes you just need to check it out for yourself and make sure the place is still standing. Remember when Jackie took over for me that time I cut my hand?"

"I do. You drove her up the wall." She laughed.

"And vice versa, I might add. Did Billy say he had a good time on vacation?"

"Yes, but that's not why I brought him up. He asked what I was doing at the office on a Saturday morning, and I told him all about Mabel Hobbs, the streaker, Harold paying the streaker—the whole nine," she said. "Anyway, Billy said that Ralph Hobbs and Zelda had a child, which is why he paid her all those years."

"Who pays child support for over forty years?" I asked. "Most men begrudge paying it for the requisite eighteen years, especially if they aren't publicly claiming the children."

"Agreed, but Billy said Ralph wasn't paying child support as much as paying Zelda to keep his secrets."

"That must be why the payments stopped after Ralph died." I poured batter onto the griddle. "He didn't care about those secrets anymore."

"Actually, the payments stopped when Zelda died, not Ralph. I should've caught that they ended before his death, but I didn't. Anyway, Zelda and Ralph died within weeks of each other. Now, are you ready for the kicker?"

"Let me guess. Harold was the child of Ralph and Zelda?"

"No," she said. "Sawyer Sykes was."

I nearly burned Ryan's pancakes when I heard what I thought I'd heard. In fact, I asked Sarah to repeat herself.

She'd said what I thought she had—according to Billy Hancock, Sawyer Sykes was Ralph Hobbs' son.

"Do you think Sawyer knew his manager paid the streaker to create the diversion?" I flipped the pancakes in the nick of time.

"I have no idea, but I think it's something the police need to ask Sawyer."

"I agree. Thanks, Sarah."

"Anytime. Keep me posted."

I promised I would, disconnected our call, and phoned Mom.

"Amy, is anything wrong?"

That's how my mother greeted me on Saturday mornings because she knew I was busy and that it was unlikely I'd call her simply to have a chat.

"No…not really." I sighed. "I don't want you upset with me again, but I have some questions about Sawyer that might be pertinent to Mabel Hobbs' murder."

Mom groaned. "Oh, honey, I don't have any love for the man myself, but that doesn't make him a killer."

"Bear with me a second. What was Sawyer's dad's name?"

"I don't know. His mother raised him alone." She paused. "I admire that," Mom continued. "I know how hard that is, since I was also a single parent."

"Did you ever meet Sawyer's mom?" I asked.

"Yes. If you'll recall, I left you with Nana one weekend so he and I could go visit her. It was so important to him that I meet her, and I felt sure he was going to propose that weekend." She barked out a mirthless laugh. "I got that wrong."

"Was Sawyer's mother's name Zelda?"

"No, it was Daisy."

"Daisy? Like, Daisy Buchanan?"

"I guess," Mom said. "The woman did love F. Scott Fitzgerald. Sawyer said she'd read Fitzgerald's books over and over."

I felt a chill despite the heat near the grill and the bacon grease popping nearby. "Billy Hancock told Sarah that Sawyer was the son of Ralph Hobbs and a woman who called herself Zelda Gerald."

Chapter Eleven

When I saw Ryan pulling into the parking lot, I plated his breakfast. The breakfast actually took two plates, but that was fine.

He gave me a wide grin as he sat at the counter.

"Dude, whatever she did to get in hot water with you," Scott said, pretending he didn't have a clue, "if I were you, I'd hope she did it again."

"No worries, man." Ryan winked at me. "I'm sure she will."

I smiled, knowing all was forgiven, and I immediately wished he could tell me something—anything—about Mr. Smith's interrogation. The café was still virtually empty, except for staff.

Pouring Ryan's coffee, I leaned closer. "Do we think Malcolm Smith was hired by the killer?"

"See?" Ryan nodded to Scott, who laughed.

"Oh, come on." I put on what I hoped was my cutest pout. "It's only us here, and we all think Mr. Smith was hired to create a diversion, right?"

"According to the man who hired Mr. Smith, the only diversion the streaker was hired to create was one to generate interest in a flagging fair." Ryan added sugar to his coffee.

"But what about—"

A group of girls from a nearby college—based on their softball jerseys—wandered in. I stopped questioning Ryan, smiled, and welcomed the team to the café. Ryan saluted me with his coffee cup, Scott went to take their orders, and I returned to the kitchen.

I knew it wasn't fair of me to try to pry information out of Ryan. But this was Aunt Bess! Sure, she was a firecracker, but she hadn't harmed Mabel Hobbs, and I'd do anything in my power to keep her from being arrested for murder.

Before Ryan left, I returned to the dining room, squeezed his hand, and whispered, "Thank you."

"She's going to be fine," he said softly. "We all know she's innocent."

It had been a busy morning, and there was no sign that traffic was letting up at lunchtime either. I barely had time to look up when Drew Hobbs came into the café, but I noticed him talking with Jackie when she went to take his order.

A few minutes later, she joined me in the kitchen.

"Well, that was weird," she said.

"What was?"

"He left."

I frowned as I flipped the hamburger patties on the grill. "Without eating his food? Was something wrong with it?" My mind raced. He'd had the turkey club, light on the mayo, heavy on the bacon, and extra tomato.

"No. He'd taken several bites before he got a phone call, tossed too much money on the table, and walked out."

"I hope nothing is wrong." I paused. "Are you sure he didn't have a complaint about the food?"

"Positive. In fact, I asked if he'd heard that the streaker had been caught," she said. "He said he had, and I told him I hoped that meant his stepmother's killer would soon be brought to justice. I mean, without knowing who killed Mabel, the authorities have no motive. Her killer could be out to get the entire Hobbs' family."

"Did you tell him that?"

She nodded. "Yeah. I mean, surely, he's thought about that. If not, he needs to. Wouldn't you want to be taking extra precautions if someone close to you was murdered and you had no idea why?"

"I guess so, but that thought could be enough to put a man off his lunch."

"Nah. It was the phone call." She waited for me to plate the cheeseburgers and fries so she could take them to her customers.

"Maybe we should pay a visit to Bella after work and try to find out if there's something going on," I said.

"Works for me."

It had been such a busy day, and I was pooped. I wanted nothing more than to go home, change into a breezy sundress, sit on the front porch, and watch the world go by.

But that would have to wait.

I'd whipped up a key lime pie for Bella, and Jackie and I were on our way to deliver it. Before she'd told him about the streaker being caught, Drew had mentioned to Jackie that Bella was still at their old home. She'd wanted to go through some of her father's things before Mabel's will was read on Monday. Since Ralph's will was primary, the disposition of his remaining assets would coincide with the resolution of Mabel's estate.

"Is Mark with Bella?" I asked.

"I don't know. I imagine so, since I can easily picture him taking everything he could get his greedy hands on." She shook her head. "If I was Bella, I'd want him to stay out of sight until everyone was over his behavior at the memorial."

I parked in the circular driveway in front of the Hobbs' home.

Bella greeted us in dusty jeans and a raggedy t-shirt. "I wasn't expecting guests."

"We don't want to intrude—just bring you a pie." I smiled slightly. "Drew came into the café for lunch today, and he told us you were here. We thought you might need a pick-me-up."

"As a matter of fact, I do. Thank you." She stood to the side. "Come on in. Just excuse the mess—I've been going through some of Daddy's things from ages ago."

"That's a bittersweet undertaking, isn't it?" I asked. "I remember going through Nana's things. Mom and I both laughed and cried a lot that day."

"I've done the same thing." Bella led us to the kitchen where she put the pie in the refrigerator. "Would either of you like something to drink? Or to eat? I still have plenty of food from the other night."

"No, thanks," Jackie said. "Is—um—is Drew okay? He left the café today without finishing his food. He got a phone call, left some bills on the table, and booked it on out of there. It concerned me."

"He's fine." Bella sighed. "Well, as fine as can be expected. I heard from Billy Hancock today that someone has retained counsel and is claiming to be an heir to Daddy's estate. This man says he's Daddy's son. Of course, I called Drew." She looked at Jackie. "Mine was likely the phone call that made him lose his appetite. Thank goodness Mark is golfing today. I'm not ready to tell him yet."

"Did Billy believe the man had a legitimate claim?" I asked, wondering why Sarah hadn't called to make me aware of this new tidbit of information. Granted, she had said that Billy was going through his mail, so there was a good chance she didn't know about it herself.

"He said he'd contact the other attorney first thing Monday morning and demand proof of paternity," Bella said. "I'm guessing this is a money grab, but Drew is desperate for the estate to be settled as soon as possible. He's afraid his business will be ruined while he waits for this matter to be resolved."

"That's right." Jackie groaned. "There can be no estate resolution while there is another possible heir—I saw that on some law show a while back."

"I tried to assure Drew that we'd figure everything out. I'd loan him the money he needs myself, but Mark and I aren't in the best financial situation either." She fidgeted with the hem of her shirt. "Do you suppose he might be able to get a loan based on what he's supposed to receive in the settlement?"

I didn't know, but I highly doubted it. Still, I nodded.

We'd barely shut our car doors before we started speculating on what Bella had said.

"The person coming forward *has* to be Sawyer, don't you think?" I asked. "Ralph Hobbs was old—how many unclaimed children could he have running around?"

"You realize you just contradicted yourself, don't you? *Because* he was so old, he could have a whole passel of illegitimate kids."

"Ugh. You're right. As much as I hate to do it, I'm going to have to have a conversation with Sawyer Sykes."

Chapter Twelve

On Sundays, Jackie and I met at the big house to prepare lunch. Sometimes others joined us, but usually it was an occasion shared by Mom, Aunt Bess, Jackie, and me. It was our weekly check-in. This Sunday, Aunt Bess was all about her Pinterest boards.

"The fair gave me so many things to pin." She clasped her hands and scrunched up her shoulders. "I put Mabel on my *People I've Outlived* board and my *Crime Scenes* board—bless her heart. And I put a link to the newspaper's article about the streaker on my *Lord, Have Mercy* board. The only thing I'm missing is something new for my *Things I'd Love to Eat* board, and I'm sure as heck not putting Mabel's pickles on there. If I wanted any of those pickles, I'd go to the store and buy me some like she did."

Mom gave her a sharp look.

"God rest her soul," Aunt Bess added. "Of course, I wish none of those things had happened—or that at least if we were going to have a streaker, he'd have been somebody that looked more like one of those Hemsworth boys—but I'm a lemons-to-lemonade kinda gal. I make the most of what I'm given."

"What have you got there, Jackie?" Mom asked, obviously desperate to change the subject.

With a side eye toward me—in my defense, I stifled my giggle—Jackie said, "Banana pudding."

"Yum!" Aunt Bess licked her lips. "You make the best banana pudding. Why don't you make it more often?"

"Because meringue is a pain," Jackie said.

"But you're so good at it." I patted her back and went into the kitchen ahead of her.

We had a pleasant lunch of chicken salad, coleslaw, baked beans, rolls, and—last but never least—banana pudding. Afterward, Mom, Jackie, and I cleared the table and tidied the kitchen under Aunt Bess's supervision.

As the other three migrated to the living room, I stepped out onto the porch and looked at the blue mountains in the distance. It was a beautiful day. Robins and doves called to each other from the maple trees and evergreens. Honeybees flitted from daisy to dandelion to

Queen Anne's lace. A monarch butterfly landed on the railing near where I was standing, and I admired its orange and black markings.

"What's on your mind?" Mom asked softly.

I turned to see her approaching with a bottle of water for me. "How do you know there's something on my mind?" I took the bottle, opened it, and took a long, refreshing drink.

"I'm your mother. I know."

"Fair enough." I had another swig of the water to buy myself a few more seconds. "I want to talk with Sawyer. Do you know where he's staying?"

She nodded. "Why do you want to talk with him?"

"Because his manager hired the streaker. I want to know if it was a publicity stunt or a distraction so he could kill the woman who stood between him and his inheritance."

"All right. Let me go inside and ask Jackie to stay with Aunt Bess. If you're going to see Sawyer, I'm going with you."

She'd barely gotten back inside when my phone dinged. I had a text from Jackie:

An errand, my butt. I know you two are going to see Sawyer. You need to let Ryan know where you're going.

I wrote back: *We'll be fine. We're going to talk, not accuse.*

The hotel where Sawyer was staying reminded me of the Bates Motel—old, rundown, and creepy. Sawyer's room did nothing to dispel my initial impression of the place. When he opened the door to us, I got such a whiff of stale pizza, beer, and dirty feet that I nearly reached for the travel perfume bottle I kept in my purse.

He stood there in the doorway wearing shorts and nothing else. "Well, this is a surprise." Giving an awkward chuckle, he said, "I'd better find a shirt before you start to think I'm planning on taking Malcolm Smith's place as streaker."

Mom and I stood outside the room and watched Sawyer pluck a t-shirt off a pile of clothes, sniff it, and then pull it on over his head.

"I'm beginning to understand what you saw in him," I muttered under my breath.

"He wasn't like that then," she whispered, but her expression was asking if he was and that she'd glossed over his faults.

"That's better." Sawyer returned to the doorway with a nod. "Don't stand out there like a couple of ninnies— unless you'd rather not come inside. And I'd really rather you didn't if you've come to tell me off again."

"We didn't." I stepped into the room. "We'd like to ask you about your mom and Ralph Hobbs."

There was a baseball game playing on the television. He picked up the remote to mute the sound. "Who told you?"

"It doesn't matter. Why didn't you come forward sooner?" Mom and I had already decided a feigned support for Sawyer could loosen his tongue if there was anything he needed to confess. "That man owed you a lifetime of everything being a Hobbs could have given you. He should have been caring for you from the time you were born."

A slow smile spread across his face. "You're serious."

"Of course, I'm serious. And I'm furious! How dare he treat you that way?"

Shrugging, he said, "It was partially my fault. When I first found out, I was hurt and determined to show him I didn't need him. I wanted to make it as a performer first. I wanted to become wildly successful and then throw it in the old man's face that the son he'd kept hidden had become one of the biggest names in country music."

That wish floated to the floor and laid heavily in the room among us.

"But that didn't happen, did it?" Sawyer's voice was ragged when he spoke again. "I can't even afford a decent hotel room. Do you suppose failure is in the Hobbs' genes and that it somehow skipped a generation? From what I understand, his other kids aren't doing so hot either."

"I think everyone is eager to get their hands on their inheritance," I said.

"I bet they are. They sure weren't going to get anything from Mabel." His face hardened as he said the woman's name.

"Did you know Mabel?" Mom asked.

"I met her." He ran his hands through his hair. "I went to her house. I told her I was Ralph's child, and I even showed her proof. Then I asked her for a loan, but the old bat wouldn't give me a dime. She said I didn't deserve anything and that Ralph's other two ungrateful children didn't either."

"That wasn't her decision to make," I said.

"No, it wasn't," he said, "but she let me know she intended to spend as much of the estate as she could before she died. The 'ingrates' couldn't get it if it had already been given to a worthy charity."

"Wow." Time to bait him and see if he was Mabel's killer. "I'd have been tempted to knock her brains out then and there. After everything you'd already been through for her to treat you that way?"

"Oh, don't you think I wasn't tempted. But what could I do?" He spread his hands. "That paranoid vulture had surveillance cameras all over the place."

Mom smiled. "Congratulations on getting the last laugh on both of them. You're going to get the inheritance you rightly deserve, and there's nothing either of them can do about it from the grave."

He looked from her to me and then back to her. "You know I loved you, Jenna. I had every intention of coming back to you after I made it big."

While Mom had his attention diverted, I reached into my purse, woke up my phone, and began recording.

"I thought we were going to be a family," I said.

"We were, sweetheart." He took Mom's hand and reached out to run his fingers down my cheek. "We still can be."

"Sawyer, did you...did you do this for us?" Mom asked. "Did you get rid of Mabel Hobbs so we could have a future together?"

Frowning, he asked, "Get rid of? I don't know what you mean."

"I'm sorry," I said. "This is my fault. I thought maybe you'd knocked Mabel out—I know you'd never intentionally kill anyone."

He squinted. "Why would I do that?"

"The people at the fair would have her taken her to the hospital, and you could convince Drew or Bella to go to the house and rip up that check."

"And then you all, as Ralph Hobbs' heirs, could get an injunction against her to keep her from recklessly spending your inheritance," Mom said. "But if it wasn't you—"

"I'm sorry, Mom. I was wrong." I shrugged at Sawyer. "I guess I was hoping you did hit Mabel with that pickle jar and that you'd done it for us—so that we could have another chance at being the family I'd wanted us to be all those years ago." I managed to muster up some tears. "I didn't mean to come here and accuse you of anything. I'm sorry." I turned.

"Wait."

I pivoted at the sound of Sawyer's voice.

"I did—I do—want us to be a family. I mean, to be honest, I didn't know when I came back to Winter Garden whether I had a chance with your mother or not, but I knew I wasn't going to let Mabel Hobbs stand in my way. I went to Drew and told him his wicked stepmother was about to put the screws to all of us."

"He helped you?" Mom asked.

"Not really, but he knew about my plan."

"Then we can pin it on him," I said.

Sawyer's jaw dropped. "Really? You'd help me?"

"You were like the dad I never had."

He blinked back tears. "Jenna? What about you?"

Shrugging, she said, "Mabel Hobbs was a bitter, spiteful woman. I worried Aunt Bess really had bonked her on the head with that pickle jar. I'm glad to know she didn't because Aunt Bess can't keep her mouth shut. She'd have put it all over Pinterest if she'd done it."

I laughed. "She would have, wouldn't she?"

"Think of what all we can do with this money." Sawyer's smile was as broad as the backside of a barn. "I can make a comeback. We can hire a nurse to stay with Aunt Bess so you can travel with me, Jen. Amy, we can grow your business too. Think of it—Down South Café franchises all over the country."

"That would be amazing." I squealed to show my delight. It was surreal that we were pretending to be so giddy over an inheritance secured by this man's bashing a pickle jar over an octogenarian's head, but if that's what it took to get his confession....

"Now, let's not get carried away just yet." Mom's was always the voice of reason, so it made sense for her to be cautious. "Are you sure no one recognized you at the fair, Sawyer?"

"Sure, I am. If they had, they'd have come forward by now. Heck, the ones who knew him didn't even turn in Malcolm Smith for streaking."

As if streaking and committing murder held the same level of severity...

"And Harold believes you had him hire Malcolm for the sole purpose of generating interest in the fair?" she asked.

"Yes." He shook his head at me. "Your mother always did worry too much."

My phone dinged, and panic must've shown on my face.

His expression darkened. "What was that?"

"Just my phone. I got a text."

"From whom?"

"I don't know," I said. "My phone is in my purse."

"Then take it out and see who sent you a message."

Recovered enough to act nonchalant, I reached into my purse, took out my phone, and saw that the message was from Ryan. "It was my boyfriend. I'll call him later."

Sawyer snatched my phone out of my hands and saw that I was recording our conversation. He called me a name I'll not repeat here and threw my phone against the wall. Then he grabbed Mom, spun her around, and pressed his left forearm to her throat.

"Please," I said.

Ignoring me, he dragged Mom toward the dresser where he took out a hunting knife. "You think I won't cut your throats and leave you here in this room? You think I won't do that for playing me for a fool?"

"Mom didn't know I was recording our conversation." It was a lie. She did know. Or she knew I was going to try to get him to confess in an audio file. "It was all me. I wanted insurance. You'd left us before—I was afraid you would again." The tears streaming down my face had nothing to do with Sawyer and everything to do with the knife he now held dangerously close to Mom's throat. "Without that recording, what would stop you from taking all that Hobbs money and never looking back?"

As Sawyer considered my words, his grip on Mom loosened slightly. I pulled the perfume bottle from my purse and went to spraying. Mom slid to the floor.

He screamed, dropped the knife, and covered his eyes with both hands. "I'll kill you! I'll kill you both!"

Mom pulled his left leg, causing him to buckle and fall backward onto the bed. I threw the nasty bedspread over him and rolled him onto his stomach. Mom hurried to the other side of the bed, folded the remaining half of the bedspread over him, and we sat on him. He kicked and fought, but we were determined. He was facing a prison sentence. If he managed to fight us off, we were facing death.

Unable to reach my phone—unsure if it was still even working—and with Mom's phone still in the car, we called for help at the top of our lungs. It seemed like forever, but it was actually only about ten minutes before we heard the glorious sound of sirens. Ryan's text had said he was on his way.

Also, never underestimate the importance of a good phone case. We got every word of Sawyer's confession, as well as his threats to murder us.

Also by Gayle Leeson

Down South Café Mystery Series

The Calamity Café
Silence of the Jams
Honey-Baked Homicide
Apples and Alibis
Fruit Baskets and Holiday Caskets
Truffles and Tragedy

Ghostly Fashionista Mystery Series

Designs on Murder
Perils and Lace
Christmas Cloches and Corpses
Buttons and Blows

Kinsey Falls Chick-Lit Series

Hightail It to Kinsey Falls
Putting Down Roots in Kinsey Falls
Sleighing It in Kinsey Falls

Victoria Square Series (With Lorraine Bartlett)

Yule Be Dead

Murder Ink

Murderous Misconception

Dead Man's Hand

Embroidery Mystery Series (Written as Amanda Lee)

The Quick and The Thread

Stitch Me Deadly

Thread Reckoning

The Long Stitch Goodnight

Thread on Arrival

Cross-Stitch Before Dying

Thread End

Wicked Stitch

The Stitching Hour

Better Off Thread

Cake Decorating Mystery Series (Written as Gayle Trent)

Murder Takes the Cake

Dead Pan

Killer Sweet Tooth

Battered to Death

Killer Wedding Cake

Myrtle Crumb Mystery Series (Written as Gayle Trent)

The Party Line (prequel)

Between A Clutch and A Hard Place

When Good Bras Go Bad

Claus of Death

Soup…Er…Myrtle!

Perp and Circumstance

Literatia Series (Written as G. Leeson)

Saving Piglet (prequel)

An Eyre of Mystery

A Tale of Two Enemies

Movie Memorabilia Series

Terminated: He Won't Be Back

ABOUT THE AUTHOR

Gayle Leeson is known for her cozy mysteries. She also writes as Gayle Trent and Amanda Lee. To eliminate confusion going forward, Gayle is writing under the name Gayle Leeson only. She and her family live in Southwest Virginia with Cooper, the Great Pyrenees in the photograph with Gayle, and a small pride of lions (cats, really, but humor them).

If you enjoyed this book, Gayle would appreciate your leaving a review. If you don't know what to say, there is a handy book review guide at her site

(https://www.gayleleeson.com/book-review-form). Gayle invites you to sign up for her newsletter and receive excerpts of some of her books:
https://forms.aweber.com/form/14/1780369214.htm

Social Media Links:
Twitter:

https://twitter.com/GayleTrent

Facebook:

https://www.facebook.com/GayleLeeson/

BookBub:

https://www.bookbub.com/profile/gayle-leeson

Goodreads:

https://www.goodreads.com/author/show/426208.Gayle_Trent

Have You Met Max, the Ghostly Fashionista?

Excerpt from *Designs on Murder*

Chapter One

A flash of brilliant light burst from the lower righthand window of Shops on Main, drawing my attention to the FOR LEASE sign. I'd always loved the building and couldn't resist going inside to see the space available.

I opened the front door to the charming old mansion, which had started life as a private home in the late 1800s and had had many incarnations since then. I turned right to open another door to go into the vacant office.

"Why so glum, chum?" asked a tall, attractive woman with a dark brown bob and an impish grin. She stood near the window wearing a rather fancy mauve gown for the middle of the day. She was also wearing a headband with a peacock feather, making her look like a flapper from the

1920s. I wondered if she might be going to some sort of party after work. Either that, or this woman was quite the eccentric.

"I just came from a job interview," I said.

"Ah. Don't think it went well, huh?"

"Actually, I think it did. But I'm not sure I want to be doing that kind of work for...well...forever."

"Nothing's forever, darling. But you've come to the right place. My name's Max, by the way. Maxine, actually, but I hate that stuffy old name. Maxine Englebright. Isn't that a mouthful? You can see why I prefer Max."

I chuckled. "It's nice to meet you, Max. I'm Amanda Tucker."

"So, Amanda Tucker," Max said, moving over to the middle of the room, "what's your dream job?"

"I know it'll sound stupid. I shouldn't have even wandered in here--"

"Stop that please. Negativity gets us nowhere."

Max sounded like a school teacher then, and I tried to assess her age. Although she somehow seemed older, she didn't look much more than my twenty-four years. I'd put her at about thirty...if that. Since she was looking at me expectantly, I tried to give a better answer to her question.

"I want to fill a niche...to make some sort of difference," I said. "I want to do something fun, exciting...something I'd look forward to doing every day."

"And you're considering starting your own business?"

"That was my initial thought upon seeing that this space is for lease. I love this building…always have."

"What sort of business are you thinking you'd like to put here?" Max asked.

"I enjoy fashion design, but my parents discouraged me because—they said—it was as hard to break into as professional sports. I told them there are a lot of people in professional sports, but they said, 'Only the best, Mandy.'"

Max gave an indignant little bark. "Oh, that's hooey! But I can identify. My folks never thought I'd amount to much. Come to think of it, I guess I didn't." She threw back her head and laughed.

"Oh, well, I wish I could see some of your designs."

"You can. I have a couple of my latest right here on my phone." I took my cell phone from my purse and pulled up the two designs I'd photographed the day before. The first dress had a small pink and green floral print on a navy background, shawl collar, three-quarter length sleeves, and A-line skirt. "I love vintage styles."

"This is gorgeous! I'd love to have a dress like this."

"Really?"

"Yeah. What else ya got?" Max asked.

My other design was an emerald 1930s-style bias cut evening gown with a plunging halter neckline and a back panel with pearl buttons that began at the middle of the back on each side and went to the waist.

Max caught her breath. "That's the berries, kid!"

"Thanks." I could feel the color rising in my cheeks. Max might throw out some odd phrases, but I could tell she liked the dress. "Mom and Dad are probably right, though. Despite the fact that I use modern fabrics—some with quirky, unusual patterns—how could I be sure I'd have the clientele to actually support a business?"

"Are you kidding me? People would love to have their very own fashion designer here in little ol' Abingdon."

"You really think so? Is it the kind of place you'd visit?" I asked.

"Visit?" Max laughed. "Darling, I'd practically live in it."

"All right. I'll think about it."

"Think quickly please. There was someone in here earlier today looking at the space. He wants to sell cigars and tobacco products. Pew. The smell would drive me screwy. I'd much rather have you here."

Hmm...the lady had her sales pitch down. I had to give her that. "How much is the rent?"

"Oh, I have no idea. You'll find Mrs. Meacham at the top of the stairs, last door on your left. It's marked OFFICE."

"Okay. I'll go up and talk with her."

"Good luck, buttercup!"

I was smiling and shaking my head as I mounted the stairs. Max was a character. I thought she'd be a fun person to have around.

Since the office wasn't a retail space like the other rooms in the building, I knocked and waited for a response before entering.

Mrs. Meacham was a plump, prim woman with short, curly white hair and sharp blue eyes. She looked at me over the top of her reading glasses. "How may I help you?"

"I'm interested in the space for rent downstairs," I said.

"You are? Oh, my! I thought you were here selling cookies or something. You look so young." Mrs. Meacham laughed at her own joke, so I faked a chortle to be polite. "What type of shop are you considering?"

"A fashion boutique."

"Fashion?"

"Yes, I design and create retro-style fashions."

"Hmm. I never picked up sewing myself. I've never been big on crafts." She stood and opened a file cabinet to the left of her desk, and I could see she was wearing a navy suit. "Canning and baking were more my strengths. I suppose you could say I prefer the kitchen to the hearth." She laughed again, and I chuckled along with her.

She turned and handed me an application. "Just read this over and call me back if you have any questions. If you're interested in the space, please let me know as soon as possible. There's a gentleman interested in opening a cigar store there." She tapped a pen on her desk blotter. "But even if he gets here before you do, we'll have another opening by the first of the month. The web designer across the hall is leaving. Would you like to take a look at his place before you decide?"

"No, I'd really prefer the shop on the ground floor," I said.

"All right. Well, I hope to hear from you soon."

I left then. I stopped back by the space for lease to say goodbye to Max, but she was gone.

I went home—my parents' home actually, but they moved to Florida for Dad's job more than two years ago, so it was basically mine...until they wanted it back. I made popcorn for lunch, read over Mrs. Meacham's contract, and started crunching the numbers.

I'd graduated in May with a bachelor's degree in business administration with a concentration in marketing and entrepreneurship but just couldn't find a position that sparked any sort of passion in me. This morning I'd had yet another interview where I'd been overqualified for the position but felt I had a good chance of getting an offer...a low offer...for work I couldn't see myself investing decades doing.

Jasmine, my cat, wandered into the room. She'd eaten some kibble from her bowl in the kitchen and was now interested in what I was having. She hopped onto the coffee table, peeped into the popcorn bowl, and turned away dismissively to clean her paws. She was a beautiful gray and white striped tabby. Her feet were white, and she looked as if she were wearing socks of varying lengths— crew socks on the back, anklets on the front.

"What do you think, Jazzy?" I asked. "Should I open a fashion boutique?"

She looked over her shoulder at me for a second before resuming her paw-licking. I didn't know if that was a yes or a no.

Even though I'd gone to school for four years to learn all about how to open, manage, and provide inventory for a small business, I researched for the remainder of the afternoon. I checked out the stats on independent designers in the United States and fashion boutiques in Virginia. There weren't many in the Southwest Virginia region, so I knew I'd have something unique to offer my clientele.

Finally, Jazzy let me know that she'd been napping long enough and that we needed to do something. Mainly,

I needed to feed her again, and she wanted to eat. But I had other ideas.

"Jazzy, let's get your carrier. You and I are going to see Grandpa Dave."

Grandpa Dave was my favorite person on the planet, and Jazzy thought pretty highly of him herself. He lived only about ten minutes away from us. He was farther out in the country and had a bigger home than we did. Jazzy and I were happy in our little three-bedroom, one bath ranch. We secretly hoped Dad wouldn't lose the job that had taken him and Mom to Florida and that they'd love it too much to leave when he retired because we'd gotten used to having the extra space.

I put the carrier on the backseat of my green sedan. It was a cute car that I'd worked the summer between high school and college to get enough money to make the down payment on, but it felt kinda ironic to be driving a cat around in a car that reminded people of a hamster cage.

Sometimes, I wished my Mom and Dad's house was a bit farther from town. It was so peaceful out here in the country. Fences, pastureland, and cows bordered each side of the road. There were a few houses here and there, but most of the land was still farmland. The farmhouses were back off the road and closer to the barns.

When we pulled into Grandpa Dave's long driveway, Jazzy meowed.

"Yes," I told her. "We're here."

Grandpa Dave lived about fifty yards off the road, and his property was fenced, but he didn't keep any animals. He'd turned the barn that had been on the land when he and Grandma Jodie bought it into a workshop where he liked to "piddle."

I pulled around to the side of the house and was happy to see that, rather than piddling in the workshop, Grandpa was sitting on one of the white rocking chairs on the porch. I parked and got out, opened the door to both the car and the carrier for Jazzy, and she ran straight to hop onto his lap.

"Well, there's my girls!" Grandpa Dave laughed.

It seemed to me that Grandpa was almost always laughing. He'd lost a little of that laughter after Grandma Jodie had died. But that was five years ago, and, except for some moments of misty remembrance, he was back to his old self.

I gave him a hug and a kiss on the cheek before settling onto the swing.

"I was sorta expecting you today," he said. "How'd the interview go?"

"It went fine, I guess, but I'm not sure Integrated Manufacturing Technologies is for me. The boss was nice, and the offices are beautiful, but...I don't know."

"What ain't she telling me, Jazzy?"

The cat looked up at him adoringly before butting her head against his chin.

"I'm...um...I'm thinking about starting my own business." I didn't venture a glance at Grandpa Dave right away. I wasn't sure I wanted to know what he was thinking. I figured he was thinking I'd come to ask for money--which I had, money and advice—but I was emphatic it was going to be a loan.

Grandpa had already insisted on paying my college tuition and wouldn't hear of my paying him back. This time, I was giving him no choice in the matter. Either he'd lend me the money, and sign the loan agreement I'd drafted, or I wouldn't take it.

I finally raised my eyes to look at his face, and he was looking pensive.

"Tell me what brought this on," he said.

I told him about wandering into Shops on Main after my interview and meeting Maxine Englebright. "She loved the designs I showed her and seemed to think I could do well if I opened a boutique there. I went upstairs and got an application from the building manager, and then I went home and did some research. I'd never seriously considered opening my own business before--at least, not at this stage of my career--but I'd like to try."

Another glance at Grandpa Dave told me he was still listening but might take more convincing.

"I realize I'm young, and I'm aware that more than half of all small businesses fail in the first four years. But I've got a degree that says I'm qualified to manage a business. Why not manage my own?"

He remained quiet.

"I know that opening a fashion boutique might seem frivolous, but there aren't a lot of designers in this region. I believe I could fill a need…or at least a niche."

Grandpa sat Jazzy onto the porch and stood. Without a word, he went into the house.

Jazzy looked up at me. *Meow*? She went over to the door to see where Grandpa Dave went. *Meow*? She stood on her hind legs and peered through the door.

"Watch out, Jasmine," he said, waiting for her to hop down and back away before he opened the door. He was carrying his checkbook. "How much do you need?"

"Well, I have some savings, and—"

"That's not what I asked."

"Okay. Now, this will be a loan, Grandpa Dave, not a gift."

"If you don't tell me how much, I'm taking this checkbook back into the house, and we won't discuss it any further."

"Ten thousand dollars," I blurted.

As he was writing the check, he asked, "Have you and Jazzy had your dinner yet?"

We were such frequent guests that he kept her favorite cat food on hand.

"We haven't. Do you have the ingredients to make a pizza?"

He scoffed. "Like I'm ever without pizza-makings." He handed me the check. "By the way, how old is this Max you met today? She sounds like quite a gal."

"She doesn't look all that much older than me. But she seems more worldly...or something. I think you'd like her," I said. "But wait, aren't you still seeing Betsy?"

He shrugged. "Betsy is all right to take to Bingo...but this Max sounds like she could be someone special."

First thing the next morning, I went to the bank to set up a business account for Designs on You. That's what I decided to name my shop. Then I went to Shops on Main and gave Mrs. Meacham my application. After she made sure everything was in order, she took my check for the first month's rent and then took me around to meet the rest of the shop owners.

She introduced me to the upstairs tenants first. There was Janice, who owned Janice's Jewelry. She was of average height but she wore stilettos, had tawny hair with blonde highlights, wore a shirt that was way too tight, and was a big fan of dermal fillers, given her expressionless face.

"Janice, I'd like you to meet Amanda," said Mrs. Meacham. "She's going to be opening a fashion boutique downstairs."

"Fashion? You and I should talk, Amanda. You dress them, and I'll accessorize them." She giggled before turning to pick up a pendant with a large, light green stone. "With your coloring, you'd look lovely in one of these Amazonite necklace and earring sets."

"I'll have to check them out later," I said. "It was nice meeting you."

Janice grabbed a stack of her business cards and pressed them into my hand. "Here. For your clients. I'll be glad to return the favor."

"Great. Thanks."

Next, Mrs. Meacham took me to meet Mark, a web site designer. Everything about Mark screamed thin. The young man didn't appear to have an ounce of fat on his body. He had thinning black hair. He wore a thin crocheted tie. He held out a thin hand for me to shake. His handshake was surprisingly firm.

"Hello. It's a pleasure to meet you, Amanda." He handed me a card from the holder on his desk. "Should you need any web design help or marketing expertise, please call on me. I can work on a flat fee or monthly fee basis, depending on your needs."

"Thank you, but—"

"Are you aware that fifty percent of fledgling businesses fail within the first year?" he asked.

I started to correct his stats, but I didn't want to alienate someone I was going to be working near. I thanked him again and told him I appreciated his offer. It dawned on me as Mrs. Meacham and I were moving on to the next tenant that she'd said the web designer was leaving at the end of the month...which was only a week away. I wondered where he was taking his business.

The other upstairs shop was a bookstore called Antiquated Editions. The owner was a burly, bearded man who'd have looked more at home in a motorcycle shop than selling rare books, but, hey, you can't judge a book by its cover, right?

I made a mental note to tell Grandpa Dave my little joke. As you've probably guessed, I didn't have a lot of friends. Not that I wasn't a friendly person. I had a lot of acquaintances. It was just hard for me to get close to people. I wasn't the type to tell my deepest, darkest secrets to someone I hadn't known...well, all my life.

The brawny book man's name was Ford. I'd have been truly delighted had it been Harley, but had you been expecting me to say his name was Fitzgerald or Melville, please see the aforementioned joke about books and covers. He was friendly and invited me to come around and look at his collection anytime. I promised I'd do so after I got settled in.

Then it was downstairs to meet the rest of the shop owners. The first shop on the left when you came in the door--the shop directly across the hall from mine--was Delightful Home. The proprietress was Connie, who preferred a hug over a handshake.

"Aren't you lovely?" Connie asked.

I did not say I doubt it, which was the first thought that popped into my brain, but I did thank her for the compliment. Connie was herself the embodiment of lovely. She had long, honey blonde hair that she wore in a single braid. Large silver hoops adorned her ears, and she had skinny silver bracelets stacked up each arm. She wore an embroidered red tunic that fell to her thighs, black leggings, and Birkenstocks. But the thing that made her truly lovely wasn't so much her looks but the way she appeared to boldly embrace life. I mean, the instant we met, she embraced me. Her shop smelled of cinnamon and something else...sage, maybe.

"Melba, that blue is definitely your color," Connie said. "By the way, did that sinus blend help you?"

"It did!" Mrs. Meacham turned to me. "Connie has the most wonderful products, not the least of which are her essential oils."

I could see that Connie had an assortment of candles, soaps, lotions, oils, and tea blends. I was curious to see what all she did have, but that would have to wait.

"I'm here to help you in any way I possibly can," said Connie, with a warm smile. "Anything you need, just let me know. We're neighbors now."

Mrs. Meacham took me to meet the last of my "neighbors," Mr. and Mrs. Peterman.

"Call us Ella and Frank," Ella insisted. She was petite with salt-and-pepper hair styled in a pixie cut.

Frank was average height, had a slight paunch, a bulbous nose, and bushy brown hair. He didn't say much.

Ella and Frank had a paper shop. They designed their own greeting cards and stationery, and they sold specialty and novelty items that would appeal to their clientele. For instance, they had socks with book patterns, quotes from famous books, and likenesses of authors.

After I'd met everyone, Mrs. Meacham handed me the keys to my shop and went upstairs. Although my shop wouldn't open until the first of September, she'd graciously given me this last week of August to get everything set up.

I unlocked my door and went inside. I was surprised to see Max standing by the window. I started to ask her how she'd got in, but then I saw that there was another door that led to the kitchen. I imagined my space had once been the family dining room. Anyway, it was apparent that the door between my space and the kitchen hallway had been left unlocked. I'd have to be careful to check that in the future.

But, for now, I didn't mind at all that Max was there. Or that it appeared she was wearing the same outfit she'd been wearing yesterday. Must have been some party!

"So, you leased the shop?" Max asked.

"I did!"

"Congratulations! I wish we could have champagne to celebrate."

I laughed. "Me too, but I'm driving."

Max joined in my laughter. "I'm so glad you're going to be here. I think we'll be great friends."

"I hope so." And I truly did. I immediately envisioned Max as my best friend—the two of us going to lunch together, talking about guys and clothes, shopping together. I reined myself in before I got too carried away.

I surveyed the room. The inside wall to my right had a fireplace. I recalled that all the rooms upstairs had them too. But this one had built-in floor-to-ceiling bookshelves on either side of the fireplace.

"Does this fireplace still work?" I asked Max.

"I imagine it would, but it isn't used anymore. The owners put central heat and air in eons ago."

"Just checking. I mean, I wasn't going to light fire to anything. I merely wanted to be sure it was safe to put flammables on these shelves." I could feel my face getting hot. "I'm sorry. That was a stupid thing to say. I'm just so excited—"

"And I'm excited for you. You have nothing to apologize for. How were you supposed to know whether or not the former tenant ever lit the fireplace?"

"You're really nice."

"And you're too hard on yourself. Must you be brilliant and well-spoken all the time?"

"Well...I'm certainly not, but I'd like to be."

"Tell me what you have in store for this place," she said.

I indicated the window. "I'd like to have a table flanked by chairs on either side here." I bit my lip. "Where's the best place around here to buy some reasonably priced furniture that would go with the overall atmosphere of the building?"

"I have no idea. You should ask Connie."

"Connie?" I was actually checking to make sure I'd heard Max correctly, but it so happened that I'd left the door open and Connie was walking by as I spoke.

"Yes?"

"Max was telling me that you might know of a good furniture place nearby," I said.

"Max?" Connie looked about the room. "Who's Max?"

I whirled around, thinking Max had somehow slipped out of the room. But, nope, there she stood...shaking her head...and putting a finger to her lips.

"Um...she was....she was just here. She was here yesterday too. I assumed she was a Shops on Main regular."

"I don't know her, but I'd love to meet her sometime. As for the furniture, I'd try the antique stores downtown for starters. You might fall in love with just the right piece or two there." She grinned. "I'd better get back to minding the store. Good luck with the furniture shopping!"

Connie pulled the door closed behind her as she left, and I was glad. I turned to Max.

"Gee, that was awkward," she said. "I was sure you knew."

"Knew?"

"That I'm a ghost."

Interested in reading more? Designs on Murder, Book One in the Ghostly Fashionista Mystery Series, only 99 cents - www.ghostlyfashionista.com

Made in the USA
Monee, IL
07 November 2022

17276436R00090